I0600134

Sea Glass Wrapped in Red

Serenity

Stacey Wilk

Sea Glass Wrapped in Red by Stacey Wilk

Serenity, Book 4

This is a work of fiction. Names, characters, places, and incidents are either the product of the author's imagination or are used fictitiously, and any resemblance to actual persons living or dead, business establishments, events, or locales, is entirely coincidental.

Sea Wrapped in Red

Cover Art by *Diana Carlile*

Published in the United States of America

Rest in Peace,
"Miss Patti Grace, ma'am."

Praise for Stacey Wilk's Books

Through the Darkness "Wilk pens a heart gripping story that will leave you breathless." *Jen Talty, USA Today Bestselling Author*

The Essence of Whiskey and Tea: "If you enjoy a good series about family and love, then this novel is sure to soothe your soul." *Booktrib*

Time Won't Erase: "The power of redemption shines in this emotional story about second chances." *Caridad Pineiro, New York Times and USA Today Bestselling Author*

Taking Root: "...multiple layers of entertainment." *InD'Tale Magazine*

Whispering Christmas: "She makes you feel deeply for each character as if you a part of the Candlewood Falls family." *Mint Copy Services*

Defining Chances: The author masterfully weaves together real-life situations, creating a narrative that's both thought-provoking and emotionally resonant. You'll find yourself rooting for Ember and Raf as they navigate their troubled pasts and learn to let go of guilt and anger. *Hidden Gems Reviews*

Chapter One

The holiday season promised to deliver miracles and boy did Skyla Morgan need one right now. Her life could be summed up as the equivalent of a piece of toxic coal in a threadbare Christmas stocking. Her fault, mostly. She didn't see the way straight to fix it, but finally, after six months of living in her car, she was ready to try.

She had driven the streets of Serenity by the Sea for two weeks and still hadn't found the courage to park and approach Bailey Russo. Terror stopped Skyla at every street corner because Bailey would have questions Skyla couldn't answer. Didn't want to answer. Yet she longed to know Bailey like a sister.

Skyla's mistakes had piled up and crushed her. She hadn't planned to end up living in her car. No one plans for that. If only... she couldn't think about the ifs now. She needed to find a place to park for the night.

Maybe knowing Bailey as a sister was asking for too

much. Bailey might not want one, but she did have one more. Well, a half sister, anyway.

Skyla cruised around some of the quiet streets. She did this every night and took in the festive Christmas lights decorating porches and twinkling in bushes. The inflatable Santas and snowmen put a smile on her face as they swayed in the breeze on postage stamp front lawns. She wanted a house one day, a place to lay her head at night behind locked doors with good heat, running water, and maybe a Christmas tree—if she dared.

She turned down the road she had found a few days ago. It was an offshoot tucked between overgrown trees that boarded the town park and the river. At first the road appeared to be more of an unpaved driveway, but once she rounded the bend, the road smoothed out.

River Road hugged the river, giving each of the three houses on it a backyard that butted up to the water. A small wooden sign on the tree side of the road claimed that the Ranger Trail began there. Or maybe it had ended there at one time, bringing hikers to the river and over the years, someone purchased the land and built three houses with riverfront property.

The first house, a small single-story bungalow style, had a lit Christmas tree in the window. The colored lights did little to provide any glow but warmed up the appearance of the house. The porch wasn't much but did offer a place to sit if the lonely rocker was any indication. One car sat in the small driveway.

The house that had Skyla's attention was the last one. It sat farther away from the other two with overgrown grass and shrubs blocking the view to the middle house which was dark and had been every time Skyla had come down the street in the past two weeks.

The last house was also small, but the property appeared to stretch wider than the other two houses. A smaller building, maybe a shed, sat behind the abandoned house. The house had to be abandoned. Besides the overgrown shrubs that climbed up to the porch railing and the side windows, the grass was also too long for this time of year, the screen door hung on one hinge, and the boards on the porch were broken through in places. Skyla had parked here two nights ago and walked around with only the light from her used cell phone.

She pulled into the dirt driveway that wasn't much more than worn out grooves in the grass and luckily on the far side of the house away from the neighbor. When she had come to check out the surroundings at night the first time, she had also walked around the house to make sure no one lived in this place. Not a single light or noise came from inside. Nothing but beautiful darkness. All the doors and windows were locked, though. Not one of the windows had a crack. She wondered if someone checked on it every now and again but couldn't be bothered with a good hedge clipper. If this were her house, she would show the quaint cottage the love it deserved.

For now, she'd settle with a decent night's sleep in her back seat. The residential area without too many eyes on her was a better choice than sleeping in a Walmart lot. She had always been safe there too, but the expansive lot with other people coming and going all night left her exposed.

She had no way to defend herself and couldn't afford to be robbed. Everything she owned, that had any value, mostly sentimental, was jammed in her car.

She needed to stretch her legs and pushed out into the damp December night. Cold wind grabbed a hold of her and shook her with its force. She grabbed her coat and slid into the chilly down. Sometimes, like tonight, she couldn't believe she had possessed a regular life with a job and... and nothing. She couldn't think about the past now. Not at night.

The ground crunched under her feet as she made her way to the back of the house toward the river. An earthy smell drifted toward her as she drew closer. The remains of a boat dock hung limp in the water. This place must've been magical once. She hoped someone would come along and restore the seashore beauty. Everything and everyone needed second chances.

If she owned a little house like this, she would have planters of flowers on the front and back porch most of the year. She'd hang gauze curtains on the windows to allow as much light as possible in during the day. She'd fix that dock and bring two chairs down for lazy afternoons with a good book. Maybe she'd plant a little garden and that one-room shed, staring back at her with dark eyes framed in white molding reflected by the moon's glow, she'd paint pink.

She liked this little town with its quaint Main Street full of shops, the ocean that bordered Serenity by the Sea in the east, and this hidden gem of a road. If she had her way, she would live here forever.

But she doubted that would happen. She'd have to get

up the nerve to approach Bailey first. Then Bailey would have to accept her. Skyla would need a real job too. Not the ones she'd had for the past year or so, the temporary gigs on construction sites, cleaning houses for the wealthy, or standing on the occasional corner where she played violin for tips before she had to sell her beloved instrument—for money.

The bitter wind blew off the water and reminded her she needed shelter. The inside of the car would be cold. She'd run the car battery for a few minutes and let the heat chase the chill away before she hunkered down under a couple of blankets for the night.

She turned toward the dark house. She could try and break in from back here. She might be slightly warmer inside and if she got lucky there was still power generating through the walls so she could run the heat and not shake and shiver all night. She'd have to move her car and hide it better, but if she was out early, before sunrise, no one would know she had slept in the house. She couldn't remember the last time she had slept with her legs stretched out. Who would it hurt if she allowed herself one simple pleasure?

Her car would have to stay in the street, but she parked at the end of the road where the pavement met the evergreens and oaks from the park. The one owner, with the Christmas tree in the window, wouldn't be able to see her vehicle even if this neighbor looked out a window. She would be fine for the night.

Skyla grabbed a few essentials, her backpack with all her important papers, including proof that Bailey was her sister, along with her two blankets, locked the car, and returned to the back of the house. With the light from her phone, she searched the windows for the best way to break the glass but decided against it. She only wanted a place to sleep, not to vandalize the house. For once, luck was on her side. The back doorknob gave way under her twist.

She hesitated. The door had been locked earlier in the week, but the need for warmth won out and she entered through the kitchen and swept the light across the room. An old-style white refrigerator hummed in the corner. Power. She couldn't risk turning on any lights. Her phone flashlight would have to do. But she did risk a quick peek in the fridge. Her stomach groaned as if to encourage her to forage. The inside was spotless but empty.

If the power worked, then she would be able to use a toilet and maybe steal a quick shower. She wandered through the other rooms. No one had been here if the layer of dust on the floor meant anything. Relief washed over her. The place was hers for a night. One glorious night.

She helped herself to the hot water in the master bath shower, dried off, and climbed into her warm sweatpants. She spread out her blanket and wished for a pillow but wasn't going back outside to dig one out of the car. She could turn her backpack into one for the night. Nibbling on a protein bar, she read a little on her phone, then slipped under the second blanket.

In the morning, she'd find Bailey Russo and tell her the truth—that she had a half sister. And maybe, just maybe, Skyla would get that Christmas miracle after all.

Chapter Two

Levi Hawkins had no one to blame but himself. He had willingly purchased the River Stone Cottage in the small town of Serenity by the Sea. The original owners had given the name to their summer retreat house that was once filled with joy, memories, and family. But that was decades ago. Now it was an abandoned house that some long-lost relative officially owned but didn't give one rat's rear end for. Levi had bought it for a song.

He had sold his home—larger and in better shape than the River Stone Cottage but echoed with loneliness—had put most of his things in storage and traveled north to New Jersey.

He wasn't sure why anyone wanted to live in New Jersey with its crowded streets, noisy beaches, and industrial polluters, but here he was. He needed to fix his relationship with his brother and that had to happen up close. Nothing long distance would repair what Levi had broken.

The GPS told him to turn left onto River Road. The

street snaked around, and the river came up on his left along with the three cabin style homes. This part of town contradicted the beach and the shops that catered to tourists. There, people filled the sidewalks and the sand. In the summer, a community of visitors stayed in tiny houses not much bigger than a tent. He had rented one for Grant a few years ago.

Only the first house on this street was occupied by an old man who had sung the blues a long time ago. At least that was what the real estate agent, Charlotte, had told him when she had introduced Levi to his new neighbor. The second house was vacant. Levi might buy that one too. Then no one could move in next door and bother him. He wasn't in town to make lasting friendships. He didn't believe in planning long-term any longer.

The only person he wanted to talk with was Grant. His brother didn't know about his arrival or the purchase of the cottage on its last leg. Grant lived a mile away on the other side of Serenity by the Sea with his wife and daughter. When Grant found out that Levi had moved into his town and hadn't told him, along with keeping a few other truths from him, Grant would be madder than a wet hen. If Levi stood close enough to his older brother when Grant discovered the truth, Levi had better duck.

The morning sun hung low in the sky and lit the river behind the little house that reminded him of something from a horror movie. He parked in his pathetic excuse for a driveway and climbed out of the car. Before he gave himself a chance to appreciate the bright blue sky and the river's view that had been worth the money he'd spent on this place, he did a mental body scan. A new habit he couldn't rid himself of nowadays. No aches. No pains. No nausea. He hadn't experienced any of those sensations in months, but the habit was ingrained as if he'd been performing the observation his entire life.

He wiped a hand over his smooth head. He liked the look and had decided to keep it. Didn't miss his hair at all. He missed other things, but not his hair.

Someone had parked an old and beat-up Nissan Sentra at the end of the street. He took in the outdated model, the faded paint, and the brittle plastic trim. The back seemed full of boxes or something large he couldn't quite make out. Probably some hiker on the trail this morning. The air was crisp, but not too cold to deter someone from taking the trail opposite his house. *House.* He tried not to laugh. This cottage standing on its last leg wasn't much of an abode.

He could have purchased a nice home on the ocean that didn't need any work, but he wasn't ready to approach Grant just yet and a buy like that would have people wondering who the new owner was.

This smaller house, away from the heart of Serenity by the Sea with its shops and beachgoers, neglected and alone on this sad street reminded him of himself. He was alone in his life now and his body had taken a real beating recently. This barren street fit him. He and the River Stone Cottage had a lot in common. Now all he had to do was figure out how to fix the thing up. Construction was not a topic he knew about. Building things by hand was Grant's department. Levi understood music, melodies, and chord progressions. He knew how to make a band succeed in the business. But fixing up a house... not a chance.

He grabbed a couple of bags out of the trunk. He'd need to purchase some furniture, or he'd be sleeping on the floor every night. Maybe that wouldn't be so bad. He had roughed it plenty of times in his life. His entire childhood had been rough. If it hadn't been for Grant stepping in front of their stepfather's fists, it would have been a lot harder.

Levi shouldn't have lied to his brother. He would do things differently if he could, but he couldn't. He had apologized a dozen times over the years to no avail. Grant was as stubborn as a swine trying to survive.

The rotting front porch wheezed under his steps. He dug the key out of his front pocket. Locked doors on this thing seemed like a waste. Who in their right mind would break into a house like this? Nothing worthwhile was inside.

He had purchased the house from photos the real estate agent had sent. He hadn't cared much about what it looked like. He wanted to live in the same town as Grant, forcing his brother to have to talk to him—when Levi was ready to face Grant. Which wasn't today. The drive had exhausted him. He still ran out of energy faster than he was used to.

The small living area had a fireplace and original wide planked wood floors covered in an inch of dust. The dining room sat empty and adjacent with the kitchen behind that. He had insisted that a new refrigerator be installed before he arrived and the utilities turned on. Sure enough, a brand-new white fridge in a vintage style waited, humming its greeting. Charlotte was as good as her word.

Three moderately sized bedrooms finished out the

house. The one in the back corner had a bathroom. He'd take that one for himself. The other bath was in the hall. Plenty of space for him. Maybe too much space.

He dumped his bags on the floor to take a look around. Then he'd figure out how to get food and the necessities he needed from a nearby town. He was pretty sure he had passed a couple of grocery stores on Route 33. He should have had Charlotte clean the place before he arrived. He wasn't as much of a forward thinker these days as he used to be.

The first two bedrooms hosted four walls and a window or two. Nothing much, but good enough if he wanted to put a desk in one or a place he could mess around with a guitar. Playing music hadn't interested him much these last months. Maybe the change of scenery would inspire him, but he didn't hold out hope. After he sold off his client base, he closed the doors on the music business.

He pushed open the door to the last bedroom and jumped.

No one had mentioned a dead body came with the place. He eased closer to the woman lying on the floor under a blanket, keeping a safe distance in case she pounced. Her face was smooth as if she were in total peace. Her long red hair fanned out around her. A worn backpack with holes in the nylon rested by her head.

He nudged her stocking foot that stuck out from under the blanket.

She stirred. *At least she wasn't dead.* Levi wiped his sweaty face. A squatter? Well, hell no. Not in his house. Not today.

"Hey." He nudged her foot a little harder this time.

She grumbled.

"Sleeping Beauty. Get up."

Her eyes flew open. She sat up in a flash, then scurried back against the wall like a spider bathed in bright light.

"Who the hell are you?" She glared at him as if he were the trespasser.

"That was my question for you."

Chapter Three

Skyla blinked, hoping the stranger standing above her would disappear, but no luck. He stared down as if she were prey that had accidentally walked into the wolves' den. Which she kind of had if he was the owner of this house.

She had meant to be out of here before the sun was up, but she must've overslept because the sun painted streaks of gold on the floor. She hadn't slept that well in a long time even if she had slept on a hardwood floor.

He could be another homeless person that had happened upon this desolate place. Not likely with those expensive shoes only inches from her face. They weren't even dirty.

She pressed her back harder against the wall, hoping it would split open, and she would tumble out into the yard and get out of there without any trouble.

Was he the real estate agent? Maybe. Whoever he was, he didn't live here. No one could have been living in this neglected place.

"Are you going to tell me who you are and why you're sleeping on the floor in my house?" He crossed his arms over his chest.

He didn't have on a coat, but the zip-up sweatshirt accented his shoulders. His jeans were wrinkled but looked new. He was of a slim build, wore being bald very well, and continued to glare at her with his charcoal eyes.

She pushed to stand but that didn't do much to take away his height advantage. "You own this place?"

"I just said that. I don't know who you are or what you're up to, but you need to get out of here before I call the cops. You're trespassing."

She couldn't argue with that. "I'm... I'm..."

"You're what? A vagrant? A runaway? Are you armed?"

"Armed? With what?" Did he think she carried a gun? She would never own a gun, not even since she'd been sleeping at rest stops and Walmart parking lots.

"Never mind. You need to get out of here."

"I'm sorry. I didn't think anyone lived here. It was only last night. I'll go." She grabbed her blankets and bag and hurried past him, catching a whiff of soap and cotton. This whole ordeal would be less embarrassing if he had a few teeth missing and smelled like mothballs.

"Someone does live here now. Don't come back." His bark nipped at her heels.

She stumbled out the front door, tripping on a jagged piece of the porch. Her things went flying. She landed on her hands and knees on the hard ground. Pain shot up her arms and legs.

"Hey, are you okay?"

She looked over her shoulder to find him standing in the doorway. The glare had softened to something more like concern. She didn't want his pity. She'd had enough pity to last her a lifetime.

"Like you care." She wiped bits of gravel off her hands.

He trotted down the steps. "I didn't mean to send you flying down the steps. You sleeping on the floor startled me. Nothing much takes me by surprise any longer."

"Whatever." She gathered her blankets and her pride from the ground.

"Do you need help?" He reached for her but pulled his hand away as if she might infect him.

Maybe you should have led with that, buddy. "I don't need any help."

"Are you homeless?"

"Like I said, I don't need any help." She forced herself to walk toward her car with a straight spine. How had this become her life, no home, no job, no options? She knew exactly how and wished with all her might she had made different choices years ago. Just one different choice would have changed everything, and she wouldn't have been caught sleeping on the floor of this guy's house.

Thankfully, he hadn't had her car towed. She didn't know what she would do if she lost the last thing she owned, the one thing that provided a smidge of safety and comfort. One day... one day she'd get back on her feet again.

"Where are you going?" He came closer but still gave her plenty of space.

She unlocked the car door and tossed her things in the passenger seat. She didn't owe this man any explanations.

She needed to get out of there before he decided to make her life more difficult.

"Are you going to call the police?" If he did, she'd have to leave Serenity by the Sea right now and never get a chance to meet Bailey Russo. Skyla would have to give up her dream of a real family once and for all. Or at least until she straightened out her life and could knock on Bailey's door with her head held high.

"Are you going to come back and rob me?"

She couldn't be sure from this distance, but his lip might've twitched up in a smile. "Nothing in that house worth robbing."

"Then I guess there's no reason to press charges for trespassing. Unless you come back and do it again."

"No chance of that. Your place is a dump." She slid into the car without another word and turned over the engine. She pulled away, refusing to look in his direction, but before she turned out of sight, she dared a glance in the rearview mirror.

He stood there, staring.

Levi watched until the old beater turned the corner. In all his experiences with rock bands, he had never walked into a place of his and found a woman sleeping in his bed or on his floor. He knew of stories where rock stars returned to a hotel room to find a couple of women hiding in the closet or bathroom, but since he was a manager and not the guy onstage playing guitar, not as many women sought him out.

Not that he didn't have women when he wanted them. He wasn't one to go long without a companion to share his bed with, but since the cancer, he wasn't interested in any woman. He didn't want to have to explain his situation.

But that woman who had just driven away might have been someone he would have pursued back in the day. Assuming she wasn't homeless. He didn't need that kind of drama in his life. He had to admit he was curious about her. She was probably around his age. What had her living out of her car?

He wasn't usually attracted to redheads, but her long, messy hair, parted in the middle as if by accident, flowed over her shoulders and hung in small waves at the top of her sweatpants. Her hooded green eyes regarded him as if he were the most untrustworthy person she had ever seen. He wasn't sure if she was sizing him up or if she looked at everyone as if she wanted to punch them. She had a lot of spunk. Scrappy. That was how he would describe her.

He shook his head. How did she get into his house? He'd have to check all the locks and have them fixed or changed. He couldn't risk an encore performance, but he did wonder if she would return just to give him hell.

He brought his bags into his bedroom. The dust on the floor had shifted under the surprise woman's blankets, making a mosaic on the wood. He disrupted the design with his foot. The first thing he would buy was a broom and sweep away all signs of her. Thankfully she hadn't left any lingering scents—good or bad—that might haunt him.

The bathroom attached to this bedroom held a shower stall, toilet and sink, leaving little room for more than one person. Water droplets stuck to the top corner of the shower. Water beaded on the shower floor. His little intruder had used his shower and left behind a bar of soap. He would need a garbage can too.

The long trip and finding a strange woman in his house had zapped him of any remaining energy. He should be mad or maybe fearful, but he was neither of those things, only fatigued. The kind that seeped into his bones, as if he'd been up for days.

His mind couldn't stay away from the woman in his house, like his tongue probing a broken tooth. Rusty—he'd call her Rusty—didn't strike him as dangerous. If she were, her instincts would have been to fight him. Instead, she ran. He envied that ability right now. He did not have the energy to run at the moment.

What he needed was a bed and a long list of supplies. Not having the house in a little better shape was a mistake. He would be the one sleeping on the dirty floor tonight.

He grabbed his laptop out of the car, then stood at the kitchen counter, creating a list of items he could purchase online and others he'd have to buy himself. At least he had thought to have the Wi-Fi up and running. A sporting goods store wasn't far from here. He could grab an air mattress for now.

Tomorrow he'd make a plan to talk to Grant and a plan to fix this place up.

He would not think about Rusty and where she was because then he might remember that once upon a time, before his diagnosis, he still gave a damn.

Chapter Four

Skyla locked the car door on a side street six blocks from the beach. Since it appeared the handsome stranger who found her in his house this morning hadn't called the police, Skyla had decided to stay in town to try and talk with Bailey today.

Walking away from her vehicle always left her in a sweat. She hated leaving her belongings for any period of time and especially when she couldn't keep an eye on her car, but her stomach continued to remind her that she hadn't eaten since sometime yesterday. She needed a meal this morning to hold her over till tomorrow, tonight if she was desperate.

She had some snacks in the car, but that wasn't enough food. She had to make the dollars from her last construction job last, but she was going to find something to eat up on Main Street where all the cute shops were.

Soon she'd find another job where the employer didn't ask too many questions. She often worked for landscapers or contractors who needed an extra pair of hands for special projects. She had become handy, fixing things around the house after Will had left her and before Emory. She clamped down any thoughts of Emory. Skyla couldn't think about Emory now.

The damp December wind whipped around the corner and settled into her bones as she turned east. She had passed a cute bakery up by the boardwalk while driving around, but the only place to park that didn't require payment was the residential side street where she had left the car.

Her belongings would be fine. What little she knew about this town was that it was safe.

The walk gave her a chance to see the small homes decorated for Christmas with reindeer on front lawns and wreaths on doors that would welcome family and friends in a few weeks for the holidays. Maybe this year she would have someone to celebrate with, but she didn't want to hope too hard. Hope had never been good to her.

The homes turned to businesses, and she came up to Tea and Tales, the bookstore that Bailey managed. A potted Christmas tree stood proud by the front door with sparkly ornaments. An oversized wreath was propped on the ground and against the door. Skyla attempted to rehang it on the hook stuck to the door, but the hook was too small for the wreath, and it landed back at her feet. Colored Christmas lights outlined the store's front window but weren't turned on. Skyla peered through the glass. No lights were on inside the store either. It didn't open for a couple of hours, saving her from stopping.

She had done a little internet research before coming to town and discovered that Bailey worked here, but the owner was someone named Luther Billinger. The website did not show a picture of this person but did show one for a Jack Billinger, climbing a ladder in what must be the back room. An action picture, Skyla figured. Jack must be a nickname for this Luther person. When she did get up the nerve to approach Bailey, Skyla hoped this Jack person wasn't working, that no one was in the store to overhear what would be an awkward conversation.

She would come back later. Right after she had something to eat. She didn't want her stomach giving her away when she announced she was Bailey's half sister. Maybe she should write a letter and slip it under the door. She had tossed that idea around a thousand times, seesawing between liking it or hating it entirely.

Skyla crossed the quiet street to Bella Notte bakery. She hesitated outside the door. Sweat slicked her palms even in the cold. Customers lingered at a table, laughing. A couple stood near the pastry case talking to someone behind the counter. Three people, well four, counting the employee. No one would know who she was here. She was miles from her old life, the life that had wrapped itself around her neck and pulled until she was out of air, suffocating. Some days she wished the snake had finished the job, but she had to always push those thoughts away. She had one reason to live —Emory, her brave little girl. Skyla would not dishonor Emory's memory by giving up. What kind of mother would she be if she did that?

On a long breath, she opened the door. Warmth greeted

her, chasing the chill away. No one looked her way, and she was grateful. She would appear disheveled, wearing the same clothes for the past three days. Not her underwear. Never that. But she hadn't stopped at a laundromat recently. Serenity by the Sea didn't have one. She had checked. But she would need to find one soon.

People often gave her dirty looks when she appeared at their favorite restaurants or cafés. Almost as if they could smell the homelessness on her. She had been like those people once, ignorant in their comforts. With confidence she didn't always have, she approached the counter and gave her order to a young man with a scornful look.

She grabbed the last open table and slid onto the chair, folding in on herself, becoming as invisible as possible. But she soaked in the adorable bakery with its white walls and black-and-white photos of what had to be generations of the same family. Dean Martin sang Christmas music from the ceiling. If she had the money, she would buy one of every colorful pastry in the glass case. Instead, she inhaled the scent of warm bread and wondered if anyone could fill up on the smell alone.

Scrolling through her phone to pass some time, she half listened to the conversations around her. She was as starved for human connection as she was food. Even being caught by the handsome stranger this morning was worth the few minutes of company.

"Someone is setting fire to Christmas trees around town," one of the men seated at the table near her said to his companion. The speaker's build was boxer-size big. His large hand covered the cup he held, and he wore a blue flannel shirt over a hoodie.

"You're kidding?" The other man had his back to her, but his size was smaller. He wore a red scarf around his neck and a black blazer. Skyla couldn't be sure, but he might have on hipster eyeglasses.

"Wish I was. Read it on the town's social media group page. The police don't know who it is yet, but they're searching. So far no one has gotten hurt." The big man's voice was higher-pitched than Skyla would have predicted.

"Some good news, then. But who would set Christmas trees on fire? What a horrible thing." The hipster leaned back in his chair.

"Someone with a lot of problems, that's who. The post said the trees were inside and outside. Can you imagine someone breaking into your house and lighting up your tree?"

Hipster shook as if the idea were too grim to imagine. "We have an alarm."

"We have some protection too. Look at the time. I have to go." Blue flannel shirt stood.

His friend followed. They waved to the men behind the counter and hurried out.

"Here's your *caffe'* and muffin, miss." An older man with an Italian accent, bright smile, and rosy cheeks placed the coffee on the table. "I added a biscotti for you. You need some meat on those bones."

"Oh, no. I didn't pay for that." She tried to hand back the long, beige biscuit.

"No." The man put his hand up to stop her. "It's Christmas. My treat. *Mangia*, yes?"

"Thank you, sir."

"Not sir. Just call me Mr. D like all my regulars. *Buon Natale*."

"What does that mean?"

"Merry Christmas." Mr. D's blue eyes twinkled, and he left her with her food.

She would make this coffee and treats last as long as possible. She didn't want to go back out into the cold. She did want to go back to that cottage, but that would be self-sabotage.

The striking man from this morning would probably have the police on her in seconds for trespassing if she returned. But there was something about that little house... She could imagine living there, fixing it up. She would paint one of the bedrooms purple for Emory. Skyla choked on her muffin. In the before life, she would have painted a room whatever color her little girl liked. But this was life after and no room would be painted—ever.

Tears burned the back of her eyes. She couldn't cry here. Mr. D would throw her out and she had nowhere to go. Her fingers played with her necklace as she shoved away anymore thoughts of pain and suffering. Better to focus on the house with its smaller guest cottage that wasn't much bigger than a large shed, but a place that size would be like a mansion to her and she would love it with everything she had left. She would tend to it, take care of it, make herself proud for once.

"Young lady?"

Skyla startled. "Sorry, Mr. D. Didn't see you there."

Mr. D had returned with the coffee pot. "Would you like more?" He offered her a simple smile.

She would love more, but not if it would cost her another three dollars. She couldn't say that, though, not to this sweet man. And she would never ask, instead going without.

"There's no extra charge." He kept his polite smile in place.

"Okay, then. Thank you."

He smelled the homelessness after all. He had to. She squared her shoulders while he poured the coffee. *He didn't know. He didn't know.*

"I overheard those two men talking about Christmas tree fires. Do you know anything about that?" If she made conversation like a regular person would, she wouldn't give her situation away. She could pretend she belonged as much as the next person.

"It's happened more than once. Disgraceful. That criminal is scaring everyone in town."

"What a rotten thing to do at Christmastime." She couldn't imagine anyone wanting to break into a house and set fire to a tree as if in some protest to Christmas.

"This world is not like it used to be. No respect for one another." Mr. D shook his head.

"I hope they catch whoever it is."

"*Sì'*. Me too." He returned to his spot behind the counter.

Skyla searched for any stories about the fires on the internet, but other than the town's social media page, she didn't find anything. Like she had heard, no one knew who was doing it or why.

She changed the search to the sweet cottage instead. It was undervalued for the area, but the building was old and neglected. She was surprised someone hadn't bulldozed it yet. Maybe that's what her stranger had planned for it. She hoped he didn't put up one of those large mansions. The cottage should stay the size it is. Perfect for one.

She would take a drive past it before Tea and Tales opened. Just to see the cute little place. Nothing more. She'd be gone before anyone noticed her, especially the owner. But having more pictures in her mind of the cottage that needed tenderness, just as she did these days, would help keep her company at night.

She tucked the reusable coffee cup into her jacket pocket, careful not to bend it, but not without a glance over her shoulder to make sure Mr. D wasn't watching her. The cup might come in handy, and she couldn't allow something with potential to go to waste.

Outside the clouds had rolled in and stole the brightness from the sky. She pulled her coat closer. Some people walked along the sidewalk in their winter coats and bright hats, pausing outside shops and peering in windows. Others strolled as if they had not a care in the world. *Oh, to be so free.* While some others power walked in tight leggings and down vests.

Wreaths hung from every street lantern and the town had added potted poinsettias in strategic places along the sidewalk. The quaintness of this beachside community called to her. It was right out of the Christmas movies she watched but never believed existed in real life. Well, certainly not her life before or after.

A woman juggled a tower of gift boxes outside Tea and Tales in an attempt to keep them from dropping to the ground. The boxes appeared to have the upper hand. She hurried over.

"Let me help you." She rescued the top of the box tower before it collided with the cement.

"Thank you. I didn't see you around all the gifts." A woman with spiral curls that bounced at her shoulders smiled, turning her blue eyes into vibrant sapphires. She wore a long belted wool coat and jeans.

Skyla's mouth dried out. Bailey Russo. She recognized her from the photos on the internet. From the bookstore's website and also from Bailey's health and wellness coaching business website. Bailey's Instagram account wasn't private and showed pictures of her and two other women with hashtags like #sistersforever and #family. The posts were from several years ago. The account wasn't up to date.

"Don't want anyone's Christmas gifts smashed." She hoped the smile was planted on her face and not sliding around all confused and worried now that Bailey stood before her.

"They're mostly books and some toys. The store is holding a drive for the holidays." Bailey unlocked the front door, then went inside.

Skyla took the action to mean she should follow. The smell hit her first, and she inhaled the deep scent. Pages and pages made from wood, filled with words pressed between decorative covers. She loved to read and had reread some of her favorites many times. When she had lost her apartment, she couldn't take all her books with her. She had sold most of them to a used online bookstore for some cash and cried the whole time. But she had kept a few and they were packed in the car.

Bailey walked toward the back of the store and flipped on the overhead lights. She set the packages down by the counter, then shrugged out of her coat.

Skyla blinked against the bright light. The shelves on the far-left wall were empty, but signs stating book categories still hung in their places.

"Are you doing inventory?"

She placed the other packages next to Bailey's but didn't get too close to the woman who was her half sister. Skyla tried to still her pulse. Here was her chance to finally tell Bailey the truth.

"We just bought the store next door. We're going to break through and expand the business."

"That's exciting." Holding her gaze to Bailey's was like looking at the sun. She had to turn away before the bright heat spotlighted the parts of her that she didn't want Bailey to know about.

"I'm sorry. I didn't even introduce myself. I'm Bailey." She stuck out her hand. The bell sleeve of her black tunic slid back, revealing a host of silver and black bracelets. She had a tiny tattoo on the inside of her wrist, but Skyla couldn't make out what it was.

"Skyla." She placed her hand in Bailey's. Skyla hadn't touched another human in months. A warm rush ran over her and tears pooled in her eyes.

"Are you here on vacation?" Bailey grabbed her phone from her purse.

"Something like that." She willed herself to say the words she had wanted to say for months, but now that she stood before her sister, Skyla couldn't do it. Not yet. She needed more time to prepare the right words. The ones she had planned on made a tinny sound in her mind and could not be used.

"We have some great events going on." Bailey handed her a flyer. The phone chirped. "That's me. Would you excuse me a second?"

"Sure." She backed away.

"And thanks for the help." Bailey turned toward her call.

Skyla took a moment to browse the shelves. She should make a run for it, get in her car and find another small town to hide in. Nothing would change if she announced that they were related. Bailey wouldn't throw her arms around Skyla and say *welcome to the family*. Skyla's whole existence said Bailey's father was a cheat and a liar. That truth would take the lead, and Skyla would be the one to pay the price.

"I can't believe it." Bailey threw her arms in the air. Her voice echoed off the walls.

Skyla couldn't pretend she hadn't heard that. "Is everything okay? Sorry. That was a dumb question."

"My best employee just called. She fell hiking and broke both her ankles. She can't work for eight weeks. What am I going to do? It's the holidays. Anyone looking for holiday work already has it. Jack is going to lose his mind. We're days away from our first Elf and Books event."

"What is an Elf and Book event?"

"Kids always sit on Santa's lap and tell him what they want for Christmas, right?"

"Sure." She had taken Emory once when she was about two to sit on Santa's lap. Emory had cried the whole time. Skyla had tried to get a picture, but Emory screamed and held out her arms for her momma. Skyla hadn't been able to stand the torture and scooped up Emory and fled.

"We're doing an elf instead and we're giving each child a wrapped book. No lap sitting. That always freaked me out. Just story time with an elf and then some coloring and a book."

"Sounds sweet."

"I hope so. Maybe I can bribe one of my sisters to do it." Bailey pressed her lips together. "It would have to be Kassidy. Maren would never go for it. If it wasn't college finals, my niece would be an excellent elf."

"How many days is this event?"

"Just one."

"I could help out." The words were out before she could stop them. What was she thinking, offering to help out here? Once Bailey found out the truth, she wouldn't want Skyla acting as anything but a grand exit.

Helping would give her some time to get to know Bailey and find the right moment to divulge the information in a tiny spoonful instead of a major dump fest.

Bailey cocked her head and narrowed her eyes.

"Forget I said anything. I shouldn't have. You don't

know me." She waved her hands as if to erase her blunder. "I'll be going. Nice to meet you."

"Hang on a second."

Skyla stopped with her hand on the knob. She hesitated, then turned. "Yes?"

"I'd have to hire you as an employee. And you said you were here on vacation."

"I am. Sort of. But I could use a little extra cash." Her mouth had created a huge problem. She'd have to fill out an application, and she'd have to lie. But the idea of a job in a bookstore, even for a short time, would be a dream.

"Have you ever worked in a bookstore?"

"I've worked plenty of retail." And she had a long time ago in high school. But in college she went to nursing school and never worked in a store again.

"Why do you want to work here?"

"I'm thinking of staying in Serenity. If this is too weird, I understand. I walked in off the street and asked for a job. Forget I said anything." She had to act as if she didn't want the job, as if the idea of it was bizarre. And wasn't it anyway?

"I'll convince Jack to go along with hiring you. I can't get anyone on such short notice. He'll want to run a background check and look at all your employment history before you can start working. You'll be great."

This Jack could be a problem if he asked her too many questions. She'd need to rehearse some answers. But if he did an internet search, he wouldn't find much about her. She had changed her last name back to Morgan before she had lost her last nursing job and scrubbed clean any of her old accounts, erasing as much of her life as possible before she ended up homeless.

"Thanks. I'm glad I can help." She couldn't keep being sisters a secret if they were going to work together.

She had longed for family and here was someone who could be that. Yet Skyla's mouth would not cooperate, would not say the words that could change her life. Because now she had a job. Something that would pay her enough money to keep her from sleeping in parking lots and in abandoned houses. Her day work kept her phone in use, put gas in her car, and allowed her to keep cheap car insurance. No money was left over for much else. But now... she might have a chance.

"I should be thanking you. You walked in like a gift from the Universe. I don't believe in coincidences. You showing up when I was about to drop all the packages was a sign. I never ignore a sign."

Skyla didn't believe in signs, but if Bailey did and that was what provided Skyla with employment, then she would tell Bailey whatever she wanted to hear.

"I'm glad I was on the street to help you. Timing is everything." She hoped her voice didn't sound as strained to Bailey as it did in her own ears.

"Where do you live? I know you're not from town, but you look familiar."

She hadn't considered there might be any resemblances. Skyla had always favored her mother, but maybe she had more of her biological father in her than she knew.

She also hadn't thought about how to answer the residence question. That would come up on a job application as well. She needed to think fast.

"Can I be honest with you?"

"Sure."

"I've been crashing with a friend. My rent went up and I couldn't afford to stay. My new place isn't available yet." If she kept piling on the lies, she wouldn't be able to remember all of them. Hopefully, in a few months, she'd have enough to rent a studio apartment. She only had to hang on until then.

"Oh, I know how that is. I've crashed on plenty of sofas when I was in between houses. My sisters never knew where I'd be at any given time. They hated it."

"But it's not that way for you any longer?" She and Bailey may have a few things in common. If and when she decided to tell Bailey the truth, those commonalities might work in her favor.

"I've been in Serenity by the Sea a few years now. I came back right after my dad died and I haven't left. Be careful. The town gets its claws in you, and you'll never leave."

"I'm sorry to hear about your father." When Skyla searched for information about Bailey after finding her name on the DNA results, she had dug deep enough to figure out Joseph Russo had passed away, leaving three daughters. That painful sentence in an obituary buried in a local paper told Skyla her biological father would not know about her.

Skyla's mother had not spoken much about the man who got her pregnant. *A one-night stand* was all she would

33

say when pushed for information. Her mother passed away a decade ago, leaving Skyla alone until she had met Will. But that hadn't worked out either. Life had left her alone too many times.

"We're having the Book and Elf event next week. I'd like to have you started by then. Can you come back tomorrow or the next day to try on the costume and fill out an official application?"

"Sure, I can." Her stomach folded in on itself. Applications asked for things like addresses and references. She had a post office box, but no references.

The door swung open, sending in a blast of cold air and three women wrapped in coats and scarves. One waved to Bailey.

"Great. I have a few things to take care of before too many customers get here. Thanks for the help, Skyla. Oh, I nearly forgot, can I have your number?"

Skyla exchanged information with Bailey, then headed out into the cold. The morning went in a direction she could not have predicted but things might work out better than she had planned.

Chapter Five

Skyla turned the car down River Road. The low sun glistened off the river's smooth surface, turning the water an opaque metal gray. She thought better of returning here a second time, but luck seemed to be on her side after meeting Bailey and being offered a job. She only wanted to see the house again as if stumbling upon it had changed her life.

When Bailey saw how helpful Skyla was, then she would be able to tell Bailey the truth and that the only thing Skyla wanted was a connection to her sisters. Bailey would be her way in to meeting the other two.

No one was outside of the first house. Another good sign. Her sweet cottage waited at the end of the road and no car was in the driveway. The house didn't have a garage, saving the worry that the stranger had pulled his car in there. She had a few minutes to admire the house before she left to locate a Walmart or campground outside of Serenity by the Sea where she could park for the night. She couldn't risk Bailey finding her sleeping in her car.

She turned the car around in the driveway, imagining that someday she would own a home like this. She wouldn't be able to explain her presence here if she were to get caught, so she put the car in reverse and headed toward the main road.

She pulled into the park where trees bordered River Road. If she walked down the trail that led back to River Road, and the stranger returned home, he wouldn't know she was there, allowing her more time to daydream about that house. She'd just sit under some trees, off the street, so no one could see her. She was good at being invisible.

A few hiking trails led away from the grassy picnic area where she parked. One of those trails would end up by her cottage. She needed to stop referring to the house as hers, but since she didn't know the name of the man who had found her, what would it hurt to say it was hers just in her head?

The trail she picked to try first was overgrown and probably not used much. This must be the one that opened up on River Road. If the trail only led to private homes, it wouldn't be a draw for hikers.

She moved aside drooping branches that scratched at her hands and face. Her feet crunched over dried pinecones, the only sound around her. Cedar scented the air because she was among a thousand Christmas trees. She missed having a tree, opening presents on Christmas morning. Her fingers went to her necklace. Nostalgia made her do crazy things like walk along a growth-covered trail to glimpse a house she would never have. But if she didn't fill her head with stories, she had no way to get from one day to the next.

She came out at the road. The driveway still sat empty. Her luck held.

She memorized the house with its shiplap side and slanted porch overhang. The corner of the smaller building poked out from behind the cottage. Weeds twisted and turned around the porch. If someone had bothered to cut those back, the house would look much better.

No one drove down the street. If she hurried, she could cut back some of those weeds and be gone in minutes. The weeds, dried and old, wouldn't stand a chance against something as simple as hedge cutters. Assuming there would be any, but she had a hunch.

That shed would probably hold things like lawn equipment, assuming there were any. But today was her lucky day. She ran across the street and into the backyard.

The shed wasn't locked. The space was dark inside. Grime covered the few windows, but she could make out that the place was basically empty. It even had a tiny bathroom in the back which surprised her.

Leaning against the wall was a metal rake. Not clippers, but she could rip out those weeds quickly. The strange man could come back and find her while she was in the middle of tearing up his landscaping. He wouldn't like it, but she had to do something for this house. Just a little something that wouldn't matter years from now. He would have a story to tell about the ghost who came along and tore out his weeds. And she would be long gone, remembering a different version of that story.

She wanted to also thank the man who hadn't called the police when he had found her asleep on his floor. Anyone else would have yelled and screamed, chased her from the house, or worse. This house needed some attention, and she could give it as a way of thanks.

If the man found her in his yard, she would have no way to defend her actions. He had told her to stay away, and she would be caught for trespassing. But she couldn't stay away. This house possessed something that touched her. Would he really mind if someone cleaned up the yard? She wasn't asking for money or anything.

She made haste and ran for the front of the house. Still no neighbors in sight. The rake broke through the dried-out earth, splintering its surface into long cracks. Thankfully, the ground wasn't frozen yet. In a month, she wouldn't be able to do this at all.

The weeds gave in to the rake's power. Vines bent and creased. The earth turned over with each pull. The sun did little to warm the day, but she broke out in a sweat and discarded her coat.

She yanked and yanked, tasting dirt on her lips until the weeds lay in tatters before her. Her arms ached from the lack of practice; it had been years since she tended a garden. She and Will had kept one, but that was ages ago. A lifetime ago. Before...

Her heart soared for the first time in months from the work. Maybe years. She wasn't cured of her struggles, the pain would never go away, but for a brief second, she forgot. The rake and the dirt pulled something free in her too. She was the Skyla of before, if only for a moment.

She had left her phone in the car and wasn't sure what time it was or how long she'd been here. She had never done anything risky like enter a man's home, take his rake, and clean his yard. This new daring side excited her.

She dragged the compost to the treed area at the edge of the property and tossed them between the trunks. The earth would take them back. She returned the rake to the one-room cottage and stole another minute to look around. A good sweep would clean this place up enough. This cottage was a palace to her.

The only thing left was to cross the street and get back onto the trail. She was almost triumphant. Two successes today. First Bailey, now this.

When the stranger came home, he would find the front of his house in better shape than it was before, and that truth was because of her. Not that he would know it. She would not return to the street or the house. One major risk was enough.

As she crossed the backyard, an engine rumbled in her direction and tires rolled over the gravel on the street. She ducked behind the house, under a window, out of sight. Her heart roared in her ears. She couldn't be found out. If he called the police after all, she would be destroyed.

The car pulled into the driveway. She held her breath, waiting for the sounds of him climbing the porch. Then she would make a run for it.

A car door closed. "What the hell happened here?" His deep voice with a hint of a Southern accent vibrated across the yard.

He must've seen the work she'd done. It wasn't her best.

She had been too quick. If she had more time, she would have been neater. She would have smoothed the land.

She would have planned for good soil to replace the old and maybe some new shrubs to decorate the area. Not that anyone could plant this time of year. But she would choose which would be best for the front of the house.

Instead of taking her time, she had rushed while she tugged and dragged. Because she hadn't had time to be gentle. She was on a crazy mission to do something for this house that did not belong to her for a man who did not like her. The Skyla she was now was out of her mind.

His footsteps pounded up to the porch. The wind came in off the river, pulsing against her, trying to give her away.

She needed to move and eased along the side of the house, just enough to dare a peek.

He stood with his back to her. His denim jeans met the tops of new work boots. His legs went on forever. His barn jacket looked new too and he wore a black knit cap on his bald head. The rugged look sent shivers over her skin more than the wind had. He had placed grocery bags on the porch and tapped away at his phone.

"Charlotte, it's Levi Hawkins. Did you send a landscaper over here?"

Levi. She liked that biblical name and couldn't wait to try it out on her tongue. Skyla hung back while Levi listened to whoever Charlotte was. At least she wasn't Mrs. Hawkins, but Skyla doubted there was one. A woman would have had this place cleaned up before she moved in.

"Well, someone ripped out all the weeds in the front.

They did a lousy job too. Do you think it could be Melvin from two doors down?"

Levi paused. Skyla fought the urge to stand up and tell him she had been the one to tear away those ugly weeds and she hadn't done a bad job, just a quick one.

"Okay. No. No. I'll let you know if I find anything else wrong. If we figure out who did this, we'll just tell them to knock it off. Yeah. Thanks." Levi ended the call.

He turned in a circle, pausing toward the woods as if the answer to his mystery were there. Skyla ducked and held her breath.

"Only in a small town like this would someone clean up a neighbor's yard and not mention they did it," he said. "I'll never get used to small-town living."

The front door closed. She counted to a hundred before taking off for the woods.

Next time she'd mind her own business.

A flash of something he couldn't make out raced by outside the living room window. Levi turned, but the flash was gone. He hurried out the front door, leaving it open as he ran down the steps. Someone burst through the cedar branches and into the woods. He caught a glimpse of flapping red material. Was that the person who had cleaned up his yard?

The sharp air bit into his lungs, stealing his breath. He wasn't prepared for the damp cold. His legs ached before he could pick up speed. He was out of practice, but ahead, the red material became a coat. He shortened the distance between them. The person was small, built like a woman. Her rusty hair floated behind her.

"Hey, wait." He continued to run along the trail, but the broken branches and twigs played tricks with him, tripping him. He had to see her again. Find out her name.

She ran as if her life depended on it. He was not in that kind of hurry. Not today. Today he wanted to catch her and ask what she was doing in his yard. He wanted to ask if she had any idea what running on these trails might cost him. His worn-out body protested.

"Hey, Rusty. Stop." He had to end the chase. He bent over, hands on knees, and gulped in wet air. If she wanted to run across the country, so be it. He would turn back, put his groceries away, and find a sporting event to watch. A fool's errand chasing her, if there ever was one.

When he straightened, he wasn't alone. She stood yards from him, a blank expression on her narrow face. Her chest heaved, but nothing else on her moved. Those red locks hung almost to her waist. Her coat dangled to the ground in one hand.

He didn't want to scare her off and stood his ground. The silent trees waited for her to move too. She didn't. She continued to stare at him.

He held up his hands palms out. "I'm not trying to hurt you. I just need to know. Were you the one who cleared the weeds away?"

She offered him nothing but the rise and fall of her chest, her thoughts locked away this time. Earlier she had given him a mouth full of spunk. What would it take to release the side of her that would sass him?

"Okay, not going to tell me. Suit yourself. But if you were the one who tore through those weeds with a vengeance, and I'm not saying it was you, but if it were, thank you."

She said nothing.

"However, please don't work on the house. I'm not looking for help."

"I didn't help you." Her voice crackled through the trees.

"That's good because you don't know a whole lot about gardening."

She fisted her empty hand on her hip. A hint of that feist he was looking for.

"Why were you sleeping in my house?" He needed to know that too. "Are you in trouble?"

She opened her mouth but closed it again. Any hint of distress and he would help her. She was alone. She had to be if breaking into what appeared to be an abandoned house meant anything.

He waited but she didn't answer him. Instead, she bolted away like a spooked deer, leaving him in silence.

He turned, defeated. The walk back brought no new understandings. A strange woman was obsessed with his house. Maybe he should call the police. But he didn't believe she was dangerous. He had looked danger in the eye. It didn't look like her.

He checked over his shoulder before closing the front door, but she had not followed.

"What did you expect?" He had chased her like an animal. She would not follow him back here and confess to why she tore up the yard. But he had to know why.

No one had ever done such a selfless act for him. She hadn't sacrificed herself or anything. He didn't need to get maudlin, but he wasn't accustomed to people providing favors without hoping for one in return.

That was why he never asked for help. He hadn't come to Serenity by the Sea looking for a handout or a special favor. He wanted to force his brother to face him. And to force himself to tell Grant about the cancer.

He tossed his jacket on the counter and unpacked the groceries.

He hadn't needed to buy a house in this town, but if he hadn't, time would have turned on its large wheel, giving him every excuse he could find to avoid Grant. The months would've piled up, and he would have lost the connection to the only blood relative he had left. After almost dying, he didn't want to leave this earth without fixing things with his brother.

Fixing this house was another thing. He took a stroll through the rooms, then landed back in the kitchen. He didn't know if he even wanted to restore this house. Maybe he wouldn't stay. Maybe he'd just walk away from it once he and Grant could move forward.

But the sad truth was, nothing waited for him anywhere else. He had no one except friends who liked him because of what he could do for them.

He hadn't asked for help in his life because he would owe, but he had become the person who everyone wanted around because of what he could give. Grant had wanted one thing from him and Levi hadn't delivered.

He went onto the back steps and watched the river. The water had no answers for him.

Tomorrow he would fix things with Grant. He would call his brother tomorrow. Tonight, he would stay put. No more running after women in the woods.

Clouds had rolled in over the river. Where would Rusty sleep tonight? He needed to stop thinking about her. She could be crazy, a drug addict, a criminal. But he didn't think so. Something in her eyes.

He shook his head and went back inside. He had one mission here in Serenity. Make amends with Grant. Chasing a beautiful woman with long red hair would not find a place on his agenda.

Chapter Six

Skyla drove out of Serenity by the Sea with the car windows down. Burning pine drifted in to meet her. Someone had lit a Christmas tree on fire. At least, she could assume after her conversation in the bakery. Such a strange way to vandalize. She stopped loving Christmas, but the idea to hurt someone else's holiday would not cross her mind. This criminal was in worse shape than she was.

As Serenity became a speck in her rearview mirror, her breath hitched, and she clutched the steering wheel as if she were in a tailspin. She wanted to be one of the lucky ones who climbed into their own bed at night in a nice home in a quiet town. After finding Levi's house, and having the connection with it, she wasn't sure how much longer she could go on sleeping in her car. She deserved better.

Her eyes burned with fatigue. The time had come to crash for the night. Driving around much longer would only make her cause an accident.

The closest Walmart was five miles away. She would

sleep there for the night. Walmarts were almost always safe, but she preferred the twenty-four-hour ones. She chose a spot under a parking lot light and got out.

She had an hour before the store closed. More than enough time to clean up and brush her teeth. Some nights she browsed, but not tonight. Tonight, she wanted to lock herself in the car and forget about the day.

Levi had almost caught her today. She was certain he would grab a hold of her and drag her back to the house to call the police. When he had stopped to catch his breath, and his footsteps no longer pounded on her heels, she had dared to see where he was. Bent in half and gasping for air. That was when she stopped.

The glass doors to the store slid open as she approached. She blinked against the bright lights and hitched her backpack on her shoulder. A picked over pile of Christmas decorations sat on the shelves right inside the doors. Christmas music piped in from the ceiling. She couldn't wait for the music to change and the shelves to be filled with something other than Christmas. Only the next holiday was usually Valentine's Day, and she didn't care for that one much either.

She took a lap around the perimeter of the store. Sometimes zig-zagging around rounders or in between aisles of shoes and socks before making her way to the front of the store where the restrooms were. She didn't want anyone seeing her go into the bathroom.

Once inside, she was quick to splash some water on her face and run her toothbrush over her teeth. At least she had showered at Levi's before getting caught. She always hurried in public bathrooms because some other women didn't appreciate her presence at the sinks. She didn't blame them. But that didn't stop the shame from burning her insides to ashes.

Did anyone think she wanted to live this way? She often wished to shout that question at the woman with her face twisted in disgust as she realized Skyla was bathing next to her.

When Skyla was a little girl, her dream had not been to live in her car, with little way to make money. It was not her dream to experience the worst possible heartbreak on earth that shattered her into a zillion pieces, turning her into someone who had no desire to breathe, let alone go to work and earn a living.

The heavy burden weighed her down day after day. Unable to deal with the loss of her child had cost her job. Two months without working as a nurse and she had lost her apartment. She had never dreamed she would be rinsing her mouth in an unfamiliar Walmart bathroom.

She hurried back into the store and then out to her car, locking the doors as she sat behind the wheel. She checked the backpack's pocket that held the paper, telling told her she had a sister in this world.

Skyla had been a part of a DNA study that rewarded her with a DNA relative. Or was it cursed?

She wished she could keep the car running all night for the heat, but she couldn't wear out the battery or waste the gas. Out of options for the day, she climbed into the back seat, left her coat on, and pulled two blankets over her. She would read until she fell asleep.

Across the lot, a bunch of young men pushed and shoved under a parking lot light. She couldn't make out any details of their clothing, especially when one was shoved out of the light's beam. Their voices carried right to her. Their words rose and fell without distinction. She couldn't make out what they said, but their body language said they were all up for a fight.

She climbed back behind the wheel, bumping her head on the ceiling as she twisted over the console and dropped into the seat. She rubbed the sore spot on her head. If those men didn't leave in two minutes, she would.

Her gaze locked on the group. Someone threw a punch. They pounced. She kicked over the engine and flew from the parking lot back onto the highway.

"What am I going to do now?" Sometimes she spoke to herself just to remember the sound of her voice.

She wasn't sure where to go, but another store was out of the question. Turning the car in the direction of Serenity by the Sea, she had an idea. It was a dumb idea, but she needed sleep.

River Road was dark and quiet. She turned off her headlights and made her way down to the end. The first house was in complete darkness. Levi had mentioned the neighbor's name was Melvin while on the phone earlier. Melvin must be asleep.

Levi's house was also dark. His car was in the driveway. She edged her vehicle between the tall shrubs at the edge of his property and the park, trying to hide. She would be gone long before morning this time. The cold temperatures wouldn't allow her to oversleep. She only needed a few hours before returning to the bookstore to help Bailey.

Once she received her first paycheck, she would find a room to rent. There had to be a place that rented rooms around here.

Skyla climbed into the back again and tucked the blankets around her. She could make out the corner of Levi's house from her spot. Knowing he was feet away gave her some peace. She wasn't entirely alone. But if he stepped onto the lawn and noticed her car, would he chase her away?

Someone like him, confident enough to run after a stranger, would be the kind of man she would want this time. She would pick with more care if a man ever came into her life again. Levi seemed like the kind of man who was worth the risk, but he would never be interested in her.

She should stop the Levi fantasies. She knew nothing about him except he was a lousy runner and seemed grumpy the two times in his company, with good reason.

Loneliness made Levi more attractive. Having no one in her life poked her hard in the ribs most days. That was her problem. She wasn't looking for a man anyway. She was looking for her sister.

She had been tempted to talk to him in the woods today, but she didn't know if she could trust what he had said about wanting to help. Running seemed like the better option.

Her eyelids grew heavy. She snuggled deeper into the seat and pictured the riverside cottage painted pink with white rocking chairs on the tiny porch and more in the back to take in the view. She imagined walking out the back door in the early morning light with a cup of coffee in her hand, her terry robe belted against her skin. She'd sink into a rocker and listen to the birds wake. She'd have plans with her sister later that day. Skyla would cook and bake, and they would sit out back and eat and tell stories.

A bam at the window startled her. She screeched.

"What are you doing out here now?" Levi leaned down and peered through the window, his hand perched to knock again.

"Go away."

"You can't stay here."

"It's a public street."

"It's freezing out here." He rubbed his hands over his arms as if to prove his point.

"Then go inside." She turned on her side and pulled the blanket over her head.

He banged on the window again. "Rusty, come inside. You'll freeze to death out here."

She pushed up on her elbow. "What did you call me?"

"Will you come inside? I'm cold, and I don't want to yell through the window any longer."

He ignored her question. Had he said Rusty? She debated on his offer. The house was a mess, but he had heat. If he wanted to hurt her, he would have by now. He was giving her a chance to spend time in the cottage she had fallen in love with. She had already lost everything. What else did she have to lose by following him?

He was halfway to the front door.

She climbed out of the car.

He was out of his ever-loving mind, inviting this stalker into his home. Doing things like this would make him a featured story on a true crime show. But his gut said she was okay, so he waited for her to cross the yard.

He had heard a car engine travel down the quiet road earlier. As the sun had sunk into the earth, the house and river noises disappeared as if someone had shoved cotton in his ears. He wasn't used to the kind of quiet that pressed on everything. He missed the bleats of the city and had been thinking about the pretzel shop down the street from his apartment when the car outside had interrupted the silence.

He had been reading by a small lamp in the bedroom when Rusty's tires crunched on the gravel. His book hadn't been holding his attention, and the inflatable mattress was uncomfortable anyway. Putting down the book and looking outside became a necessary option.

Now, he stopped at the bottom of the front steps. She had slid from her covers in the back seat of her car and faced him, her jaw set. It appeared he had won the first round.

Won what, he did not know. Or why he wanted to win anything with this woman in the first place. He had plenty on his plate with moving to this town in secret. He needed to speak with his brother before someone spied him and told Grant. Or worse, Grant found him.

"You can sleep on the air mattress," he said over his shoulder. Which left the floor for him. His body would protest the hard and cold floor in the morning, but he hadn't been the one sleeping in a car. He could suffer for one night.

Good thing he had purchased a broom. His furniture should arrive later in the week.

Her footsteps hurried behind him. He didn't turn around until they were both inside and he had closed the door.

"Why are you sleeping in your car?"

"What did you call me before?" Her gaze scanned the room. She stayed by the door.

"You answer my question first. Is someone after you? Are you running from the police? A fugitive maybe?" He should have thought about those possibilities sooner. He wasn't in the business of harboring a criminal. He'd had enough of his own troubles with the law in his day. He didn't need to revisit any of that at this stage of his life. But she still gripped his curiosity.

Her lip twitched up in a small smile. "That was three more questions."

"Fine. Answer all four of mine and I'll answer four of yours." If she wanted to play games, he could play too. He liked games.

She dropped her backpack on the floor, then slipped off her coat and tucked it under her arm. The material was worn in spots, old and tired from long-term wear. Her gaze dropped to the floor before finding his again, but she gave nothing away. Her lips pressed into a thin line, and he wasn't sure if she was going to answer him.

Anytime he had crossed paths with someone who looked as if they slept in a car or on a bench, they were dirty, missing teeth, or muttering to themselves. She was none of those things. If she was on the street, he suspected the time hadn't been long.

"Have you decided not to play along?" He crossed his arms over his chest. He wasn't ready to give in too much to this stranger. He did need some answers.

She blew a large breath over her lips. "I sleep in my car because I'm homeless. That should be obvious, Einstein. You saw my car packed to the hilt. No one is after me. I'm not running from anything. I have never committed a crime. Are you happy now?"

"Is that one of your four questions?"

"No." Her eyes darkened.

He would give her some slack. He had invited her inside, after all. "Thank you for answering me. I'm sorry to hear you're homeless. What happened?" He was sorry. No one deserved that. When he and his brothers were kids, they had almost ended up on the street a couple of times. Their stepfather spent his money on booze instead of the rent.

"It's my turn to ask you questions." She remained by the door.

"Fair enough." He wished he had a chair or something for her to sit on. Coming here unprepared was the dumbest thing he had ever done besides lying to Grant. That was pretty stupid.

"Why did you invite me in?"

"Because it's too cold to sleep in your car. You don't have to stand by the door. I won't hurt you."

"Let me be the one to decide that. Why did you chase me today?"

"I wanted to know if you were the butcher who went after my weeds." He took a seat on the floor. The day had worn him out. Fatigue ached in his bones. He needed a good night's sleep and doubted he would get one with her here. Another thing he hadn't thought about. He really should be less impulsive.

"Your yard looks better now." She tilted up her chin.

He fought the laughter bubbling in his throat. "I disagree."

"We'll agree to disagree. Your yard needs a lot of work as does this house. You should take better care of it."

"Noted. Any more questions?"

"What name did you call me before?"

"Rusty."

She arched a brow.

"I won't make you use up a question. I didn't know what to call you when I thought about you after I found you sleeping on my floor. Your red hair made me think of the color rust."

Pink splotches bloomed on her neck. She tugged her hair close to her face. "My name is Skyla."

"Prettier than Rusty. You have one more question, Skyla."

"Who are you?"

Chapter Seven

"My name is Levi Hawkins. I just moved into the River Stone Cottage which is why this house looks the way it does."

"You named your house?"

"It came with a name. I asked you to come inside because I can't watch you sleep out there. Though, I'm not sure you're even allowed to sleep in your car on the street." He removed the knit cap and wiped a hand over his head.

She wondered how he wasn't sweating. He hadn't removed his coat either and the tiny house was warm. Deliciously warm.

"If a resident notices that my car doesn't belong in the neighborhood, they usually call the police, and I have to move. But on a street like this, with only a couple of houses, I'm safe for the night."

"Sounds like a tough way to live. If you don't mind me saying." He finally hung his coat up on the peg by the door.

"And if I do mind?" She didn't mind at all. Living in her

car wasn't exactly easy. She just needed to keep some kind of upper hand so as not to be completely pathetic.

"My apologies, ma'am." He tipped his head.

"Where are you from? Because that's not a Jersey accent."

"Down south."

She was curious about his decision to buy this vacant house in a place he wasn't from, but she would save that question for now. He had been gracious enough to pull her in out of the cold.

"Thank you for asking me in. Tonight would have been rough out there. The temps are dropping." She hated to admit that she needed his help. Maybe because he was a stranger, she could be more honest. It didn't matter what he thought of her. Soon, they would never see each other again.

"I bought some groceries. Are you hungry? I could whip us up some eggs. I make pretty damn good eggs."

She was starving. "I'm fine. Thanks. Could I use your shower again?"

"You don't want to eat? Suit yourself. You know where the shower is, but I'm hungry. You can watch me eat."

"Whatever." After he had offered for her to come inside, the prospect of sleeping in her car broke her heart. Night after night reduced to nothing more than a beggar. She had never begged. Not once. And she debated on telling him that. She wasn't just some worthless person who had squandered every opportunity put in her path. Life had beat the crap out of her and won. But she had earned her way, made money or did without. The past six months had stolen what little pride she had and left her wrung out and wasted. That part she would not tell him, and she would never mention Emory.

Skyla grabbed her bag, then locked herself in the bathroom, turned the water up high, and stripped out of her clothes. Might as well make the most of the hot water. She washed her clothes too, then left them on the curtain rod to dry.

She dried off with her scratchy towel and dressed. She could stay in the bathroom all night. This small space offered more comfort than anywhere else she had been recently. Except Levi's bedroom floor.

She couldn't hide out in the bathroom or spend the night in this house. This whole scene was crazy. She and a stranger bunking together like old friends. She should go.

"Skyla, are you okay?" His voice was far away, not right outside the door.

He must be giving her some space. How did he know she needed it? If she had to guess, he must need some too. Why buy a house out here by the river where no one lived except some old guy? From Levi's clothing to his expensive car outside, money didn't seem to be an issue. He could probably purchase a house that had at least seen the wet side of a sponge lately.

"I'm fine. I'll be right out." She took a deep breath and opened the door.

He waited at the end of the hall by the living room. His denim shirt was untucked. The top two buttons were undone, revealing smooth skin and a small tangle of chest hair.

"The air mattress is in the master bedroom. You can sleep there."

"No, that's your room. I'll be fine in one of the other rooms with my blankets. Shoot. I left them in the car."

"I'll get them." He turned to go as if the blankets should be retrieved this second.

"No, thank you. I'll do it." She did not want him rummaging around in her back seat, witnessing up close the destruction of her life or the tattered remains.

"Suit yourself but take the big bedroom. There's a bathroom in there too. I thought you'd use that one."

"I didn't want to impose."

"I think we're past imposing. I invited you here. Let's go into the kitchen. The eggs are on the stove."

She followed him. The kitchen smelled of sulfur, but at least the stove tucked into the corner worked. The pan looked brand new. He worked the spatula while she took a spot at the opposite end and leaned against the wall.

"We'll have to stand to eat. Sorry about that. I'll order some things online tonight and have them here tomorrow. Just a folding table and chairs for now. Nothing fancy."

"Why are you being so nice to me?" She wanted a warm bed to sleep in and a hot meal, but she couldn't believe this guy was offering up his food and his home without wanting something in return. She didn't dare utter the possibility that he might want to sleep with her in exchange for his kindness. She had been down that road before, had to fight to be free without harm, and wasn't going to live through that again.

"I don't know. You seem like you're in trouble and I'm

tired of thinking about my problems. I figured I could help you out a little and then help myself from thinking all the time." He handed her a paper plate filled with scrambled eggs.

She hesitated. He pushed the plate closer. She took it and had to control the urge to stick her hands in the eggs and shovel them down her throat. He gave her a plastic fork and a smile as if he understood her ravenous need to eat anything.

"What kind of problems do you have?" She shoved a forkful of food in her mouth. The eggs burned her tongue, but she didn't care. They were fluffy with the right amount of salt.

"Too many things to list, but one of them is buying this house in the shape it's in. I had to be out of my mind when I bought it. I'm kind of regretting it now." He leaned against the counter away from her and crossed his ankles.

"So, why did you?"

"Long story. But the quick version is I wanted to live near my brother."

"That must be nice to be close with your brother." She had no siblings. After her mother died, she had been alone except for Emory. Then after Emory, Skyla didn't see the point in going on without anyone in her life, but maybe if she had a brother or a sister who could have been a shoulder to lean on, she wouldn't be in this mess.

She wanted Bailey to accept her in the worst way. Skyla didn't want to walk through this life alone any longer. A sister. A family. A blood relative. She could almost reach out and grab hold of everything she ever dreamed of having, but she would not put her fist around any of it. Telling Bailey meant she could lose this new job.

"We're not close. He hates me."

"I doubt that if you moved to his town." If she had a sister, she would try hard not to fight over the small things families get caught up in.

"Trust me. When Grant finds out I'm here, I had better be fifty yards away. Why do you live in your car?" He speared his eggs and kept his gaze on his plate.

His quick subject change threw her off-balance. She gobbled up the last of the eggs and placed the plate on the counter to give her more time before answering.

"Like you, it's a long story." How could she tell him about all her mistakes?

"I have all night."

"But you didn't tell me your story." She glanced over at the pan and wondered how much he would care if she scraped the sides for one more bite.

"Another night." He reached for her plate. "Damn. I forgot garbage bags. I'll have to go out in the morning."

"Why did you pick this house? There had to be others for sale."

"I didn't want to be near the heart of town and only one other person lives on the street. I'm not up for socializing these days."

"But you invited a stranger into your home." She couldn't figure this guy out. On one hand he didn't appreciate what he had in this house and on the other he was the most generous person she'd ever met.

"Yeah, well, you looked in worse shape than I am." He offered up a shrug and a wry smile.

She couldn't argue with that.

"Are you going to fix the place up?" She took in the kitchen with its old wood cabinets and small snack bar that faced the dining room on the other side. If this were her house, she'd paint the walls white and expand the window over the sink to let more light in and the view of the river. She'd buy a small table for two so she could sip coffee in the morning as the sun came up over the water when she wasn't sitting outside in her imaginary rocking chairs.

"Maybe just enough to live in it through the holidays."

She peered out the door but couldn't see anything except a wall of blackness and Levi's reflection in the glass.

"You aren't going to stay here permanently?" She whipped around to study the expression on his face. He must be joking about not staying for long.

"Depends on what happens with my brother."

"Let me get this straight. You bought a house that you don't want and might not stay in which means you'll what? Sell it? Then move somewhere else?" She had never been so carefree with money.

Growing up, she and her mother always struggled to make ends meet. Skyla had never known who her father was because her mother never admitted to anything more than a one-night stand while on vacation with her girl-friends. Once, after insistence from Skyla, her mother admitted the man who was her father had been tall and handsome. Mom hadn't known his last name.

"I don't know what I'm going to do with this house. I

could rent it out or sell it, but I'm not up for the project of fixing it up. I didn't think about that before. I wasn't thinking about much before."

Her mother had terrible taste in men. Each one had gone in and out the door as if it revolved on crack. They all left behind heartache and bills. Skyla had become a nurse to have a steady paycheck and be in a field that always needed workers. She liked helping people too. She liked it so much she had become a maternity floor nurse. She had loved her job until Emory... Her thoughts never gave her any peace.

"You're rich. Aren't you?"

"Why are you asking me that?"

"That car you drive for one and for two, no one with the kind of money problems I have would dream of buying a house they weren't going to live in for a while. I can't even afford rent. I can barely afford to eat. You know what, I think I'd better go. Thanks for the eggs."

Levi didn't know how good he had it, and that turned the heat up in her veins, searing her. She stormed past him, but he gripped her wrist.

"Hang on a second. I'm not judging you. I don't know what you did to end up living in your car. For all I know, you brought your problems on yourself, or you tour the world spinning on your head and you like living in your car."

"Everyone judges someone like me." She grabbed her backpack and her coat. Cold air assaulted her the second she stepped outside. Her hair was still wet from the shower. Now she'd freeze all night and would have to find another place to sleep. She couldn't stay on his street.

She should just leave town and never come back. Everything was wrong. She searched for her keys in the backpack but came up empty. Her stomach hollowed out. Had she locked them in the car? She cupped her hands on the sides of her face and looked in the back seat. She couldn't see anything and went back to rummaging through her bag. Her fingers gripped cold metal, and she could breathe again.

"Skyla, wait." Levi's voice fell like an icicle on her head.

"Go away." She dropped the keys.

"I'm sorry. I'm doing this all wrong. I really wanted to help you. Not send you out into the cold night. Come back inside. I won't ask any more questions."

"No, thank you. I'll be fine." She had managed this way for the past six months. Something would change now that she had a job. It had to. Christmas was the time of miracles, and she was due. She dropped to her knees and swiped the keys out from under the car.

"Do you like living in your car? If you do, just say so, and I'll go back inside and leave you alone. But if you would rather sleep in a warm house, then come with me. At least I have heat."

She struggled to meet his gaze. "I hate sleeping in my car, but I don't know if I should accept your invitation this time."

"Please. I'm a moron. I know. Stay the night. Sleep on a warm mattress. In the morning, if you still want to go, you can."

"I'm not staying more than one night." Tomorrow she would tell Bailey about the DNA test. If things went well,

Skyla would find a way to stay in town, but if Bailey rejected her, then Skyla would leave town. New York City wasn't far. She could try her hand there.

"That's up to you, but I hope you'll change your mind."

"Why's that?"

"I need someone around here to help me clean up the place some. Inside and out. I could hire you, pay you. Then you wouldn't be taking a handout from me, and I could have this house in better shape while I'm here. You did a great job with the weeds. The house could use your touch."

"I don't want your pity." She should shut up and take the offer, but she didn't. This man with his wealth and Southern accent thought he could swoop in and save her. She would save herself.

"I don't pity you. I would never do that. But I know what it's like to struggle without any way out. I grew up poor. I got my lucky break when a man who worked at a pretty popular music venue gave me a job sweeping floors. I finally had some money and a way into the music business. Without his help, I might be living in my car too."

She forced her face to stay neutral. "You probably made that story up right now."

"I did not." He held up his hand.

"You said I did a lousy job with the weeds." She was running out of excuses to say no.

"I've changed my mind. What do you say? Will you take the job?"

"I don't know." Two jobs in one day? Santa had never been this good to her.

"Come on. Do you have any other better options?" He arched a brow.

"Well, actually, I just took a job at the bookstore."

"That's great. But my job comes with room and board. Is the bookstore giving you that?"

"Well, no, but starting tomorrow I'll sleep in that cute little shed in the back."

"Have you been in that shed?"

"Yes. That's where your rake was."

"You used a rake on the weeds? Well, that explains a lot. Look, you won't be sleeping in the shed. There's no floor. It's dirt. Mice have moved in, and a stiff wind comes in off the river and right through the walls. You're bunking with me."

"What will your brother say when he finds out you're allowing a homeless person to live with you?"

"He'll say it's about damn time I thought of someone other than myself."

"Selfish, are you?"

"The worst kind." He gave her that lopsided smile.

"Good to know."

"Skyla, I promise that you will most likely hate me by the time you're done here. Everyone does."

"I doubt that." She couldn't imagine how anyone would hate a man like Levi who had generously offered her a place to stay and a job without wanting anything in return. Whatever was brewing between him and his brother was probably not much more than a sibling misunderstanding.

"You'll see."

Chapter Eight

Skyla hesitated outside Tea and Tales. The store wasn't open for another ten minutes, but the lights were on, and someone moved around in the back. From the angle, the silhouette resembled a female. Most likely Bailey, but Skyla needed another minute to gather her nerve before going inside. She began employment today, and fear rattled her insides.

Circumstances in her life were changing like a sudden storm, and she wasn't sure what needed securing in place and what could be left alone. She had rushed out of Levi's this morning. After she woke, she had made a bowl of cereal, assuming the still sleeping Levi wouldn't mind. But the walls had pressed in on her, as if that new storm tried to force its way in.

Levi would have more questions she didn't want to answer yet. He might even decide to take his job offer away, and she wanted, no needed, the extra money. With both jobs, she'd be on her feet faster. The new year just over the horizon showed promise.

He had insisted she take the mattress last night and after a few minutes of debating, he had grabbed her backpack. Panic had robbed her senses. She almost lunged at him, ready to scratch his eyes out for taking what belonged to her, but he had plopped the bag in the main bedroom without so much as glancing at it. Then he closed himself in the room across the hall. He had been unaware of the rage inside her. He had truly wanted to help. At that point, she had given in and slept one full glorious night on a mattress.

With all the turbulence, she needed a little time to pull herself together. Now that she had been out of the house for a while, she was ready to work for him. He had promised to purchase cleaning supplies and gardening tools today, but that would be later.

An icy wind blew in from the ocean, pushing her forward. She pulled her coat closer. No more stalling. She had work to do. The knob gave way under her hand. Of course, the bookstore would be ready to accept customers early. The stores on Main Street were the kind of establishments expected in a small town like Serenity. If Skyla couldn't make a life here, she would find it hard to leave.

"Good morning." Bailey waved from the register at the back of the store. "You're an early bird."

"I hope you don't mind. I had extra time this morning. I thought I'd come help wrap those books and maybe try on the costume." Skyla inhaled the sweet book smell and settled some of her nerves.

Bailey's warm smile washed over her, releasing more tension. Bailey wore a tie-dye headband in a style that reminded Skyla of the seventies. Bailey's black turtleneck sweater had cutouts on the shoulders and the arms flowed past her wrists.

"I would love some help." Bailey clapped her hands. "Come on over here. Give me your coat." Bailey gripped her shoulders and slid the coat off with ease.

"Thanks."

"You have to try this new tea I had brought in from Japan. I can't wait for the store next door to be ready and open. Having a huge counter for coffee and teas along with seating is going to be amazing. We're so crammed in here right now." Bailey led her over to a coffee station filled with sweeteners, stirrers, and napkins. Milk carafes sat to the side, waiting for someone to come along and make use of them.

"I'm fine. Really. You don't have to fuss." But Bailey placed a hot cup of green tea with scents of mango into her hands.

"I can't believe my luck, finding you. I told my sisters how I manifested extra help in the store even before Amy got hurt. We need to hire people this time of year, and then there you were. Like magic. Don't you love it when something like that happens?"

"I don't believe in manifestation." If wishing for something to happen actually worked, she would not be suffering alone right now. She would have her husband and her child in her life. She'd still be working, helping women bring babies into the world instead of breaking down every time a woman delivered a child. If manifestation had worked, Skyla would have been able to convince her boss not to fire her.

"Really? I can change that." Bailey wiped the air with her hand.

"I don't think so." She sipped the tea and burned her tongue.

"I've made a believer out of many a skeptic." Bailey laughed. "Your necklace is pretty."

Skyla's hand reached for the thin gold chain. "Thank you. It's a family piece."

"I love that. My family only has hordes of sea glass. If you're ready to start working, I have a pile of books in the back that need to be wrapped. You can drink your tea back there. Wrap as many as you can in the next two hours. We'll start slow until Jack meets you, and if you're here at lunch, we can order food in."

She wouldn't be spending money on food today. She'd skip lunch and eat dinner at Levi's since he said his job offered a place to sleep and some food. Once she started making a couple of dollars, then she might be able to indulge in three meals a day. She'd have to pretend she was one of those people who went hours without eating.

"Bailey, there's something I need to tell you." She couldn't do it. She couldn't pretend to be someone she wasn't. She couldn't come here day after day and not tell Bailey they were related. The whole purpose of her trip was to find her family. Bailey would understand. She didn't seem like the kind to judge.

"Oh no. You aren't bailing on me already, are you? If you don't want to wrap all those books, I can find something else for you today."

"I wasn't going to say I'm leaving. I'm grateful for the job."

Bailey wilted. "Thank the gods. Okay, what did you want to tell me, then?"

She could do this. Saying the words didn't have to be hard.

The chime above the door rang. The cold air whisked in and interrupted them. A tall man with light-brown hair that swooped up in the front swaggered through the door. He reminded Skyla of a younger Kevin Bacon.

"Bailey, you are not going to believe what happened. Oh. I'm sorry. I didn't see you. I'm Jack Billinger." This man, Jack, came toward her with his hand out.

His shake was firm and formal. This was the man in Bailey's life. The one who would do all the background checking. The one who had the power to blow Skyla's plans out of the water if he thought the homeless woman was up to no good.

"Jack, this is Skyla. The woman I told you about." Bailey looked between her and Jack.

Jack stopped. He tilted his head and considered her. "Yes. I remember. Thank you for helping Bailey with the packages the other day."

"It was nothing."

"What brings you to Serenity?" Jack fished his phone out of his back pocket.

"Visiting a friend." Now she could say that with a

straight face. Not that she and Levi were friends, exactly. They were more like employer-employee. But that was close enough.

"That's wonderful. Anyone we know?" Jack looked to Bailey as if she had the answer.

"I doubt it. He just moved to town." Serenity by the Sea might be a small town, but not so small that Bailey and Jack would know Levi or his brother. That would be insane.

"You'll have to bring him by. I love meeting new people," Bailey said.

"I know Bailey spoke with you about employment, but what are your qualifications? Do you have any references?" Jack tapped on his phone. "I don't mean to be rude. I'm taking notes."

She froze. He was the kind of guy who wrote everything down and never forgot a thing. "I've worked retail before, but it's been a while."

"What about references? Our application has a spot to write them down. Did Bailey give you an application?"

"Not yet." Bailey arched her brows, but Jack seemed oblivious to whatever message Bailey was sending.

"We really need to have that on file and the references complete before you can be on the payroll. I don't pay under the table."

"Jack, we'll take care of the formalities. I need someone to help while Amy is out." Bailey gave him a soft shove, but her eyes were void of playfulness.

"Of course, but this is still a place of business. I'm sure you understand, Skyla."

"I wouldn't want to do anything to harm the store." Or herself. This job circled the drain. She should be used to losing by now.

"I'm sure you don't, and since Bailey spoke so highly of you, I'm certain you'll work out just fine. Without the application in place, the store could be liable for any problems caused by you or done to you. That's all I'm saying."

"I'll get her the app this morning," Bailey said.

"And what about references? Can you provide at least one?" Jack's fingers hovered over the phone.

The real answer was no. After Emory... Skyla had tried to return to work, but watching babies born and parents filled with love, hope, and joy, Skyla found herself crying in the supply closet when she should have been tending to her patients. She had pushed her boss too far one day, leaving him no other choice but to fire her.

"Sure thing. I mean everyone has references, right?" She hoped her forced laugh sounded genuine.

"See?" Jack said to Bailey. "She has references and there's no problem." He turned back to her. "Thanks for understanding."

All she could offer was a nod in response. Now she had lied and didn't know what she would do to come up with a solution. If she told the truth about her situation, they would send her on her way. And if she told Bailey now that they were half sisters, Bailey would wonder why Skyla didn't tell her that first.

Jack turned to Bailey again. "I came by to pick up the plans for next door. I'll grab them and head over there to meet with the contractors. Then I have some Christmas shopping to do. I'll see you tonight."

Bailey wrapped her arms around Jack's middle. Jack pulled Bailey to him and kissed the top of her head. These two loved each other very much. Any fool could see that. Skyla wasn't certain Will had ever looked at her that way. He never really loved her and that was why he walked away after Emory.

"Don't forget I have s'mores with my sisters." Bailey placed a kiss on Jack's lips.

Skyla looked away and went back to sipping her tea.

"Right. Goodbye, Skyla. If you could bring those references in as soon as possible, that would be greatly appreciated."

"Sure. No problem."

"It was nice to meet you." Jack hurried into the back, then returned with rolled-up papers. He strode out the door, leaving the cold air inside.

"What's s'mores?" She was curious and wanted the conversation away from her.

"My sisters and I get together once a week to have s'mores and talk stuff out. We try for once a week at least. Sometimes life gets in the way, and we have to push it off."

"That sounds like fun."

"It is. So, what were you going to tell me before Jack burst in here?"

"Oh, that. I wanted to tell you I'm staying in town through the holidays. I'm here for whatever you need."

"That's really sweet, Skyla. Thanks. It's so nice to meet genuine people this time of year."

If Levi hadn't already driven out of town to purchase what he needed for his house from Walmart, if his head didn't pound because he hadn't eaten anything, and if his lower half didn't ache, he would not be entering the Hammer Home Hardware Store right this moment.

In fact, he wouldn't be here ever or until he had a chance to speak with Grant. But he had been out all day, buying cleaning supplies, gardening tools, and home goods. His low back was on fire. He needed to go home and take a nap. But he couldn't return without the safety glasses or the lightbulbs. Skyla couldn't work without those glasses. He wouldn't want her to get hurt and she did want to start as soon as possible. Which was a good thing, because they couldn't go on living in that mess.

The lights in the ceilings at River Stone Cottage were mostly burned out. Until he purchased a few more lamps, they needed to be able to see better in the dark and since darkness took over around five o'clock every day, they needed light.

He stepped inside Hammer Home. It smelled of grease and wood. A thin layer of dust coated the floor. Most of the metal shelves were stocked full of power tools, nuts, bolts, screws, latches, keys, and hooks. In the back was signage leading to building materials and electrical supplies.

A man came out from the back room and stood at the counter. "Can I help you?"

The man was average height with a halo of brown hair and a salt-and-pepper goatee. He sported a hardware store apron and offered a friendly smile while he wiped his hands on a faded cloth.

"I need two pairs of safety goggles and some lightbulbs."

"What kind of lightbulbs?"

"The kind that go in the ceiling." He wouldn't know one kind of lightbulb from another. As long as it screwed into the ceiling or a lamp, he was fine with it. He had an old girlfriend who had tried to tell him which ones were better for the environment, but since she was usually on the side of complaining about each and every thing in her path, he hadn't paid much attention.

"Need to be more specific. You've got your halogen, incandescent, and fluorescent. Then we've got soft white, bright white, and true white. There's a cool tone light color that some of my regular customers enjoy."

"You pick." He had borrowed trouble by coming in here and really wanted to skate out before he was noticed by anyone who might recognize him. His sister-in-law or one of her sisters could come prancing in here any second. He also knew Grant's neighbors, Kate and Howie who lived a few doors down every summer in one of those tent contraptions. Kate had been hounding him for months to come visit.

"Which room do you need this for and what's its purpose?" The guy typed away at an outdated computer held together with duct tape.

"Does it matter?" A burst of cold air hit him from behind. He turned to find the door closing. A guy with puffy blond hair snuck down an aisle. Levi let out a long breath. No one he knew.

"Of course it matters. Are we talking recessed cams or accent lighting? Will the bulbs go in a wall sconce or a ceiling fixture?"

"I didn't think buying lights would be this difficult. Recessed. Hallway and kitchen."

"I'll grab what you need from the back. And those safety goggles too." He turned to go but turned back. "You're not from around here, are you?"

"What makes you think that?"

"I know everyone in Serenity. Worked in this hardware store with Ralph, the owner, for the past six years, and that accent you have isn't Jersey."

"You're right. Just moved to town."

"Welcome." The man stuck out his hand. "Name's Todd. My wife Ellen and I live a few towns over in Wayside. If you need anything at all, just ask. This is a friendly place."

Levi shook. "Nice to meet you, Todd. I'm Levi."

"You look familiar." Todd narrowed his eyes.

"I have that kind of face." If Todd knew everyone in Serenity, then he would know Grant and he and his brother looked enough alike that someone with a good eye might notice.

"I'll be right back with your items." Todd disappeared into the back.

Levi took in the store. A plastic menorah was propped on the counter with none of the blue lightbulbs lit. Hanukkah didn't start for another week.

On the far side of the store, there were Christmas decorations and a couple of decorated trees on display. He never had a tree growing up. When he could afford his own, he'd hike out to the tree farm and cut one down himself. When his career took off and money wasn't an issue, he had purchased a fourteen-foot tree for his two-story family room and paid a company to come and decorate it. Maybe he'd get a small tree this year. Skyla might like it. If he had to guess, celebrating Christmas wouldn't be on her recent list of accomplishments.

The door swooshed open, bringing in more cold air. Levi wasn't sure he'd ever get warm this winter. The ocean's wet air went straight to his bones.

A man, average size, with a stocky build, strode toward him. His lips were pressed into a thin line as he narrowed his eyes. "Evening."

"Hello."

"You new in town?"

"What makes you ask that?"

"I'm the captain of the Serenity by the Sea fire department. Kevin Wright." He stuck out a meaty hand. "I know everyone in my town. It's my job."

Levi shook with some hesitation. Kevin Wright gave his hand a hard squeeze. "That's some grip you have there, Mr. Wright."

Kevin Wright gave him a stiff nod. "Call me Kevin. Is Todd around?"

Before Levi could answer, Kevin shouted, "Todd, are you here?"

Todd appeared as if he stood just inside the back room

door. He beamed a smile at his customer. "Kevin, how's it going?"

"Good. How's the family?"

"Everyone's doing well. Ell—"

"Glad to hear it. Do you have more of that twine? I'm almost out."

"I do." Todd turned to Levi. "Kevin runs the Christmas tree lot in town. You should get your tree from him."

"Good to know."

Kevin offered that stiff nod again. "We're on the corner of Seawinds Way. Can't miss us."

Kevin paid for his purchase but stopped right before he opened the door. "Todd, you might want to take that tree out of the window. Not sure what the arsonist is going to do next."

"I heard he's only lighting real trees on fire," Todd said.

"For now. Evening." Kevin left the store.

"I'm sorry. I haven't grabbed all the bulbs. I'll be right back." Todd hurried away again.

If Levi had known purchasing a few items would have turned into an event, he would have skipped it. All he wanted was to go home and sit on that air mattress. He didn't want Skyla to have to sleep on the floor, but his body needed something softer tonight.

He leaned against the counter and debated on shouting to Todd to forget the lightbulbs. They'd manage with the couple he had and come back tomorrow.

The door swung open again. Another gust of cold air blew in, but this time the customer had the power to stop his heart.

"What the hell are you doing here?" His big brother, Grant, glared at him from his spot by the door. Grant's piercing gaze said Grant had come no further in forgiving him.

"Hello, Grant."

He should've waited on the safety goggles and the bulbs. He didn't need them tonight, but some strange force brought him here. The force was a redhead bunking at his house and he had wanted Skyla to see he had done everything he could today to make her comfortable.

Why he needed to make her comfortable was beyond him. Nothing he did where she was concerned made any sense to him. The chemo had really screwed with his brain. That could be the only explanation.

If he had gone straight home after the shopping and put his feet up for some rest, he wouldn't be standing there facing Grant with nothing to say.

"Why are you here, Levi? What would make you come to Serenity when you aren't wanted."

"I moved here." Might as well get it out on the table.

"You did what? You had better be joking because I've made myself clear. We're through." A vein pulsed on the side of Grant's neck.

"I just want to talk." That was all he had wanted from the moment he had confessed what he had done, but Grant had shut him out.

"I don't want to talk to you. And if I did, you didn't have to move here to do it. The phone still works."

"Yours doesn't." He had tried to call Grant at least a

hundred times. Grant never picked up or returned a single call.

"I don't want to talk to you. I don't want to live near you. My family is here. I don't want them near you either."

"You cut your hair." He and Grant had the new look thing in common, though Levi was certain Grant hadn't changed his look due to cancer.

Grant blinked. "I... what's that got to do with anything? I told you three years ago to stay out of my life, and I meant it."

"I'm not going anywhere. I bought River Stone Cottage on River Road. I'm staying. You'll have to get used to it. Moving here was one way to force you to talk to me."

"I've got those lightbulbs." Todd came out of the back, holding a box of bulbs up over his head. He stopped cold. "Grant, nice to see you again."

Grant nodded but never took his gaze from Levi. "Todd."

Todd glanced between the two of them. "Do you two know each other? Because I can cut the tension with a chainsaw. Take it outside if someone's going to throw a punch."

"Grant is my brother."

"Didn't see that coming. Okay, I still don't want any fighting."

"No one's going to fight here. Levi is leaving," Grant said.

"I'll give you two a minute. I forgot something in the back anyway." Todd slipped into the back room.

"I'll head out so you can do your business, Grant. You have to talk to me sometime. You can't stay mad forever."

"Sure, I can. I don't want to see you around. You see me coming, you go the other way. Got it?"

The store heated up like a brick oven or bumping into Grant unexpectedly had gotten the best of him. Sweat broke out on his back. He took off his coat and with two fingers, he flipped it over his shoulder. The stifling warmth still overwhelmed him, leaving him little choice except to take off his hat too. He slid the knit cap from his head.

Grant took a step back. His eyes grew wide. "Is that some new music look?"

"Something like that." Now wasn't the time to tell Grant about the cancer and the treatment. Levi was in remission. Testicular cancer had a very high success rate. The doctors had told him if he was going to get cancer, this had been the best one to get. He hadn't seen the point in arguing with the docs that no kind of cancer was the best one to get. Or how no man wanted to give up a testicle.

He would tell Grant about the disease and the treatment when his brother was less pissed at him. Levi didn't want pity to be the reason they spoke again. He wanted Grant's genuine forgiveness.

"What music group are you lying to now?"

"I'd rather not do this here. I was planning on coming by in a few days to tell you I'm in town."

"Well, now I know."

"Yeah. Look, I'm sorry. I'll always be sorry for lying to you. I hope someday you'll forgive me. Someday soon because we don't know how much time we have left."

"Don't go getting philosophical on me. It's not your style."

"Could you tell Todd I'll be back tomorrow for the stuff I asked for? I've got to be getting on." He needed some fresh air before he fell over. His muscles ached too. Some days he still fought the fatigue and other days he could run a marathon.

"Tell him yourself."

"Come on, Grant. Just tell him." Levi headed for the door.

"I'm not your messenger."

"Never said you were." He pushed outside before Grant could say something that would draw him back inside the store.

The sun was about to set and draped the west in blankets of oranges and yellows. The cool air soothed his heated skin but did little to combat the weariness in his bones.

Levi walked the half a block to the beach. Most of the stores on Main Street had closed for the day. Even this time of year, when darkness swallowed everything in its path, the tourists didn't come out at night to shop. He had learned that when he had researched this town for Grant several years ago.

Levi had known Grant would love it here and he had. Levi had loved it too, but he hadn't stuck around because he had screwed up again with his brother. He had lied to Grant's wife. His brother and Kassidy were just dating then. Grant hadn't invited him to the wedding because Levi had almost ruined everything for a chance at a good business deal. A deal that had benefitted him the most.

The wind picked up off the ocean. The scent of burning cedar came to him on the breeze. He searched for a bonfire on the beach but found none. Someone had set a fire somewhere, but he would not find it.

Needing a few minutes to pull himself together before he returned to that dump of a house and Skyla, he leaned against the metal railing separating the boardwalk from the dunes. He wanted his face free of any evidence of his conversation with Grant. Levi didn't want Skyla asking questions.

He hadn't expected Grant to still be furious. Maybe a little mad, but Levi had hoped once Grant saw him in person, he would remember all the good times they shared, of which there had been plenty, and ease up some. The man held a good long grudge.

Three women walked with flashlights near the water's edge. The crashing waves drowned out any sounds, but their bodies bent in ways that indicated they were laughing.

One woman bent down and picked something up, then threw it in the water. Maybe they were searching for sea glass. Grant had said Kassidy and her sisters did that all the time. The women were too far away, and it was too dark to know for sure, but those three were probably the Russo sisters. They were bound together like a clockwork spring. And as feisty as razor wire.

Skyla reminded him of them in that way. She had a lot of spitfire in her too for someone who was down on her luck as much as she was. He admired her spunk and her resilience. Life could scrape away every ounce of hope and come back for more like it had a right to steal your soul.

He needed to get away from the beach and go home before someone else saw him. He'd buy the things he needed from the hardware store somewhere else, somewhere out of town.

He'd give Grant more time to cool down, and then he'd try again to fix what he had broken. He hoped Grant would find a way to forgive him. Levi had lost enough time, and he didn't have any extra. No one did.

Chapter Nine

She couldn't believe she had lied to Bailey. What was she thinking? Skyla paced the tiny cottage with her hands in her hair. Levi wasn't home yet, which she was glad about. She needed to find a way out of her situation before he returned. How could she tell him what she'd done?

She had promised references to Bailey and Jack, and she had none to give. They weren't going to allow her to work at the store now and she wanted a chance to get on her feet and then tell Bailey about the DNA results.

Because at the end of the day, job or not, Skyla deserved to know who her father was. If he was a man that Bailey and her sisters respected, would never believe he was capable of having a child from an affair, she didn't want to be the one to ruin his image, but she wanted to see if her interest in playing the violin had been from him. She wasn't very good at it, had only played in the high school orchestra, but she loved that instrument and had hoped that one day she'd get to play it again. That was before she had to sell it to survive.

She wanted to know if her father liked spicy food the way she did or if he was someone who helped people when they were in trouble. She was tired of being alone in this world.

Skyla checked out the window, but only the dark night stared back at her. She had expected Levi to return by now. Hopefully he was okay. She went into the kitchen to drum up something for dinner. He had a can of soup she could heat up for them both.

She used to dream about a grandparent for Emory when her daughter was first born. Skyla would hold Emory in her arms, rocking her in that beat-up chair Will had found on someone's curb, being tossed for garbage. She'd sit there at night with the moonlight streaming in and make up stories for Emory about the best grandparents in the world. She'd talk about a grandfather who would play with her in the yard, come to her school events, brag about his grand-daughter to anyone who would listen.

Had her father been the kind of man who rooted for his children, supporting them in everything they did?

The front door swung open, startling her. Levi dashed in on the cold wind with bags in each hand. His cheeks were dotted pink. She came around from the kitchen. The living room warmed up with his presence. She let out a long breath at the sight of him.

"Sorry I'm late. I thought I'd be home sooner." He put down the bags, then slipped out of his coat.

"You don't answer to me. But I'm glad you're back." And she was. She wasn't used to being in a house alone anymore. Her car was like a cocoon, protecting her. Many nights she would have given anything for a room with four walls and a roof, but now that she was here, the house echoed and groaned against the wind, spooking her.

"I see you swept the floor. It looks good." His eyes were wide and sunken, outlined with purple bruises, but still held a warmth.

"I had a lot of energy to burn when I got back. I cleaned the kitchen too. I wiped down the cabinets, the counters, and the oven. The inside of the oven was spotless like no one had ever used it."

"You work fast." He leaned against the wall and closed his eyes.

"Are you okay?" She placed a hand on his arm. His bicep was toned, but small. Heat rolled off him like he might have a fever.

"Fine. Just tired." He smiled, but it didn't reach his eyes. His drooping lids confirmed his proclamation of fatigue.

"I've got some soup on if you're hungry." She hoped he wasn't getting sick, but if he was, she would tend to him. She still had nursing skills, and she owed this man so much already.

"Soup sounds great."

"I wish you had some furniture for us to sit on." She grabbed the bags he had put down and brought them in the kitchen.

"Coming the end of the week. Sorry I didn't order that card table. I forgot." He followed her into the kitchen.

"No problem. Fancy dining for me is sitting in the passenger seat instead of behind the wheel. I guess we could stand at the counter to eat."

"We could bring the blankets out here and light a fire."

"Like a picnic. I'll get the blankets. You sit." She looked around as if a chair might appear. "On the floor, I guess. Or I can drag the air mattress into the living room."

"The floor will do. I bought more groceries and things we'll need. If you give me five minutes, I will unload them. I grabbed some dinner rolls. They'll go with the soup."

She almost laughed at their dialogue. They spoke like an old married couple who had lived together for decades when they were really strangers to one another.

"I'll do it. I need to feel useful since I'm not paying rent." She would earn her keep. She always had until recently.

"I'm paying you to fix the place up. Remember?"

"Still not paying rent, Levi." She nudged him back into the living room, then ran and grabbed her blankets to spread on the floor.

She went through the bags, putting staple items in the cabinets and perishables in the fridge. She smiled to herself as another fantasy of doing this night after night with Levi popped into her head. She always had stories running around in her mind. One day she should write them down.

What they needed was a sofa, a kitchen table, and real mattresses to sleep on. Well, he did. She peeked into the living room. Levi had started a fire and was now sitting on the floor, leaning against the wall with his eyes closed.

"If you'd rather take a nap, I could wake you or put a bowl in the fridge for when you're ready."

If she had to guess, he was recovering from what had to be cancer treatment. She'd seen enough patients at the hospital to recognize the drawn look. But she wouldn't pry. He would have to tell her his story, if he ever wanted to share.

He glanced at her. A wisp of a smile crossed his lips. "I'm no good, Skyla. You should think about that while running around trying to help me."

She came out from the kitchen. "No good how? Because what I've seen so far is you're kind and generous. You let a stranger into your home. I could be a serial killer."

"You don't give off that vibe."

"That's good to know." She hadn't met too many people who took kindly to a homeless person. Levi was a rare one. "So, tell me. What's wrong with you?"

"I've done some selfish things in my life. I've hurt the people I care about."

She went back into the kitchen. They could continue the conversation from separate rooms. She needed to keep her hands busy. If he was gearing up to throw her out, she wanted something to hold on to when it happened.

"I'm sure whatever you did, you didn't mean it." She washed two new bowls and then poured soup into each.

"Sometimes I did what I did because it would benefit my business. I didn't care about anyone else." His deep voice vibrated against her skin.

She turned to find him in the doorway, leaning his shoulder against the jamb. "Why are you telling me this?"

"Because I want you to know who you're shacking up with."

"Are you trying to get me to leave? Because if you are, just say it. I don't have to pretend to make you dinner, clean your house, or any of this stuff if all you're going to do is throw me to the street. I'll go now." She held his gaze.

"I don't want you to leave. I want you to stay."

"Then what are you getting at? Because I don't care about your past mistakes. I've got plenty of my own."

"I ran into my brother today and it went as bad as I expected it to."

"Oh, I'm sorry to hear that." Seemed like they both had bad days with their siblings.

"Do you know what I kept thinking about after?" He came farther into the kitchen. The warmth in his eyes deepened. The space between them sizzled with something electric.

"No, how could I?" She put rolls into another bowl to give her hands something to do.

"I kept thinking I wanted to get back to this sad excuse for a house and you."

"Me?" She dropped a roll.

"Yup. I never thought I'd say that." He retrieved it from the floor and tossed it up and down like a ball.

She had imagined that Levi would want to come home to her, but the things she dreamed about never happened. That was why they were just her little fantasies that kept her going on lonely nights.

"That's very nice of you." She didn't know what else to say.

"There's something special about you."

"I'm not special. I'm the opposite." She was a grieving mother, divorced, mostly jobless, homeless. Nothing special about any of that. No one would trade places with her.

"I don't see it that way." He leaned his elbows on the counter.

"I think the cold has frozen your brain. Would you like a salad with the soup? You bought enough stuff I can throw together a small one."

"I can make the salad."

"Levi, you should sit down. You look pretty tired."

"I'm okay."

"Are you sick?" She wasn't going to ask, but she couldn't stop the instinct to help when someone looked as if they needed it.

"I don't know. My skin is hot, but I'm cold too."

She went to him and pressed a hand against the side of his neck. "You're burning up. You have a fever. Did you have any acetaminophen?"

"'fraid not, ma'am." He swayed on his feet.

"Okay, cowboy. You're going to lie down in the main bedroom on the mattress. I'll cover you with a few blankets, and then I'll run out and get some."

"There's money in my wallet."

"I don't need your money for that. I have some." Spending on a bottle of fever reducer would use up her entire allowance for the week, but she wanted to do this for him.

He gripped her wrist. "Don't allow your pride to get in

the way. Take my money. Take all of it. Rob me blind. I don't care. The money doesn't matter anymore."

"I think the fever is making you say weird things."

She helped him onto the mattress, then yanked off his boots. She covered him with three blankets. He shivered.

"I know it's none of my business, but it might be better if I knew. Did you have cancer?"

"I did."

"Could this be a side effect from your treatment?"

"Nah. My treatment ended five months ago. I just didn't bother to grow my hair back." He gave her a thin smile.

"You don't need it. You carry bald very well."

"Thanks. I think I might close my eyes for a little while."

"That's a good idea. You sleep. I'll get what you need, and then I'll be back."

"Skyla?" His voice was a whisper.

"Yes?"

"Use my money. Don't spend yours. Promise me."

She could only give him a small nod. Tears had sprung up and if she opened her mouth, she might burst.

Skyla found a twenty-four-hour drugstore outside of town. She was grateful that she wasn't likely to run into Bailey unless she too needed medicine at this hour. Skyla bought Levi the acetaminophen, a thermometer, tissues, and a few other items he might want. He was paying, after all. She navigated the streets, pushing the speed limit. Getting pulled over wouldn't do her or Levi any good. She slowed as she crossed the town line into Serenity.

If she lived in this town, she would never want to leave except for the occasional emergency. Serenity had everything she could want, charm, history, the ocean, the river, friends and family. She tucked her hope inside her heart. Now she needed to get inside and check on Levi.

He was asleep. She put the back of her hand on his forehead. He was still hotter than she liked but she wouldn't wake him yet. Rest would work wonders on him.

She put some of the soup in the fridge for him, then reheated some for her.

With her own money, she had purchased a one-inch Christmas tree figurine. It had been marked down several times and forgotten about in a bin by the register. She had grabbed the little tree, hoping it would perk up Levi. She placed it near his eyeline so when he woke, he'd find it and the fever reducer waiting.

She went out to her car and dug around for the picnic blanket she used when she spent time outside whether during the day or at night. She didn't often sleep outside alone, but every once in a while, she found a camping lot filled with RVs and friendly people. If the weather was right, she might go to sleep looking at the stars with the ground under her. She could pretend she was on a fancy hiking trip. She would sleep on that blanket tonight. She also had one more fleece blanket. Tomorrow she would ask

Levi if she could unpack some of her stuff and store it in the extra bedroom.

Was she planning on staying? How could she? She had lied to Bailey and Jack about her references. No, she couldn't unpack as if she and Levi were building a life together. This was just one of her fantasies. Levi wasn't hoping to save her from a life on the street. He had offered a way for her to make some money. As soon as she was finished here, he would send her on her way. He had warned her off him, after all. Best to remember that.

She settled down in the extra bedroom across the hall. If he woke and needed something, she would hear him. But she wouldn't sleep. She wanted to be alert if he needed help.

A noise startled her. She hadn't remembered falling asleep, but she must have because the moon no longer spilled through the window, where it had left ribbons on the floor.

One second she thought about Levi across the hall and now she woke to the pitch-black room.

"I didn't mean to wake you." His voice came from inside the room.

Her fingers searched for her phone, then turned on the flashlight feature, pointing the glare away from his face. "Are you okay? Do you need me to get you something?"

"I couldn't sleep. I took the acetaminophen. Thank you for leaving that and thank you for the tree." He sat on the floor with his back against the wall, far enough away that she would not have accidentally bumped him if she had rolled over.

She stole a glance to the corner of the room where she had left her backpack and clothes. Nothing had been touched.

"It was nothing. What are you doing in this room?" Not that she minded the company. She could listen to the cadence of his voice all night if he were inclined to speak without stopping.

"You were having a bad dream, so I came in here to check."

The noise that had startled her awake was probably her and not Levi coming in the room. Sometimes the nightmare of losing Emory played like an old movie with grainy film and a creaking soundtrack, invading her sleep and what little peace she could gather when she closed her eyes. She had often woken in the car, screaming. There she never had to worry about waking anyone. Even before she lost her apartment, when she woke covered in a cold sweat, with her heart demanding to be set free with each pound, no one else lived with her. Will had left her only moments after they had lost their girl.

She wished that each time she had the nightmare, someone somewhere in the dark unknown would subtract from the total times she would face that hell until she hit zero. But no such mercy existed. She was doomed to suffer in her sleep too.

"I woke you. I'm sorry." Even in the dark, she couldn't face him.

"No, I was up for a while. Do you want to talk about it?"

"Not really." Not ever.

"I understand that. I don't like talking about the stuff

I've been through either. What's the point? No one cares. They have their own garbage to dig through."

She could agree with that. In some of her worst times, she had looked around and found herself alone. Anyone she knew had their own lives with their own troubles. They didn't want to borrow hers or help her hold up the weight of what life had piled on for her.

"I reheated that soup you left. Another thank you."

Even with the little beam of light, his smile was visible, but his eyes were hooded. He still wore the clothes he had fallen asleep in earlier. He was crumpled and she wondered if he would be more comfortable in something other than jeans. She had to reprimand herself. Thinking about Levi and his long legs in any way other than a man giving her help would only land her in a hurt of trouble.

"You don't have to keep thanking me. You're paying me to do a job." She placed her phone against the wall, allowing the light to recede the darkness without blinding either of them.

"That's to take care of the house. Not me."

"You come with the house."

"Tell me what brought you to Serenity by the Sea. It can't be the job opportunities." His soft chuckle floated to her in the dark.

"I found your job offer, didn't I? And one at the bookstore. The job opportunities have been plenty for me."

"Two jobs. That's impressive." He shivered as if someone walked on his grave.

"Wouldn't you be more comfortable back on the mattress? Sitting on the floor isn't good for you."

"Thank you, Nurse Skyla, I'm okay."

"You must be cold. Or your fever is back. Let me get you a blanket, at least."

"How about if I come over there and we share yours."

Before she could answer, he pushed off the floor and settled by her. He smelled all male and a hint of cedar. He lay on his side and propped his head with his hand. His smile danced in his eyes as if he was used to having his way, and she assumed he was. A man with that kind of confidence to make himself at home beside a woman he hardly knew couldn't often hear the word no.

"You're avoiding my question. If you don't want to talk about why you picked Serenity by the Sea of all the shore towns on the East Coast, it's no skin off my nose. I am curious, though. Who are you really?"

She wanted to share her reasons with him for coming to town and that scared her. She hadn't trusted anyone since Will left her. Now she had a strange man sharing space with her and he brought her comfort like no one else.

She couldn't explain the pull Levi caused in her. But she had to tread with caution because if he found out her real reason, that Bailey was her sister, he could use that information against her. She couldn't risk losing the job and the future opportunity to tell Bailey the truth.

"I really am Skyla Morgan from Montague Township."

"Where is that?"

"The tip of New Jersey. Our township is so small we don't have any traffic lights."

"That's small. Were you looking for some place bigger

and landed in Serenity? This place must be a metropolis compared." Gravel filled his laugh.

"It kind of is. There are two traffic lights here at the border of town."

"Okay, Skyla Morgan of Montague Township, tell me something else about you." He let loose a wide yawn.

"It's late and you should rest." She had to be at work in the morning and needed some sleep too, even if talking with Levi in the dark held more interest than sleep.

"I'll rest when you tell me your real story. I came here to force my brother to talk to me. Why are you here?"

She hesitated, then on a deep breath, she told a partial truth.

"I took a DNA test several months ago as part of a study that paid and found out I have a half sister. I tracked her down to this area on the shore. Somewhere in Monmouth County. I found Serenity, started driving around, and liked what I saw. When I discovered your street with what I thought was two abandoned houses I figured I could hang out here and no one would be the wiser." She wouldn't say who the sister was for now or that she had tracked her down right in Serenity. Let him think this sister could be anywhere in the county.

"Have you spoken to her?" He turned onto his back, looking up at the ceiling.

"Not yet. I'm trying to find the right time." She followed his lead. Her eyes grew heavy. Levi seemed as if he had a second wind and would talk for the rest of the night.

"What are you waiting for?"

"She might not want to find out that her half sister is

homeless and living in her car." She wouldn't have during her life before. Skyla reached over and turned off the flashlight. The darkness swallowed them whole. She was grateful since her truths were cut in half and she didn't lie well.

"You don't know that. She might be thrilled to have a sister. I think it would be cool if another sibling showed up out of the blue. In fact, I'm surprised one hasn't." His gravel-filled laugh turned into a cough.

"Let me get you some water."

"I'm fine." He gripped her wrist. His heat seared her skin.

She settled back down. "You are one of the few people who isn't scared by homeless people."

"You aren't like the stereotypical homeless person we see on city streets."

"Give me another year. I will be." The day she walked around filthy because she couldn't bathe, wash her clothes, or brush her teeth loomed like a rattlesnake ready to pounce. She needed a future and a chance. Levi might be able to help her get started, but would he be brave enough?

"You make light of your situation." His words slowed and drifted away.

He must be falling asleep. He needed the rest and so did she, but she had to ask before this moment passed. In the light of day, she would lose her nerve, and it would be too late.

"Could I ask you something?"

"We're roommates now. Why not?"

"In order for me to begin working at the bookstore, I

need to provide a reference. I understand if you can't or don't want to, but it would be a huge help and I don't have anyone else to ask in town and I know you already offered me work, but—"

"You want me to be a reference." He turned, facing her, any trace of sleep gone from his voice.

"I know it's a lot to ask, but I'd like to work there too."

"Will it get in the way of your work here? There's a lot to do."

"I can work around the stuff you need here. I hope you'll understand, but if you're not comfortable with it—"

He gripped her arm. Her words stopped short, but she didn't want him to let go.

"You talk a lot."

"Only when I'm nervous."

"You don't have to be nervous around me. I thought we were past that part."

"Yeah, well, I'm still me. And we've only known each other a couple of days."

"I'll be a reference for you, but we'll have to figure out how you would've worked for me and how we're both in this small town at the same time."

"We could say I'm your assistant. Or was. Or something."

"That might work." He shifted to his back again. "I'm beat. Let's get some sleep. We can talk about it in the morning."

"I'll go in the other room so you have some space." She pushed off the floor.

He gripped her arm again. "Would you be more comfortable on the mattress?"

"You should sleep there. You're probably still fighting that fever. I can help you get across the hall."

"I'm not going anywhere unless you come with."

"Levi, that's not necessary. I'm fine here."

"Fine on this drafty floor? It sucks in here." He pushed up off the floor in one fluid movement. He grabbed the blankets and marched out.

She stood staring off in the direction he went even though it was almost too dark to see.

"Grab your phone and join me," he said from the other room.

She couldn't sleep on the mattress next to him. Being next to him moments before had sent shivers over her skin and she wasn't sick with a fever.

He was right about the drafty floor though, hard and uncomfortable. And she did need a good night's sleep. She'd slept in a chair in a patient's room on more than one occasion. Staying in the room with Levi would be close to that. Of course, those patients were babies and that was a lifetime ago. This was crazy.

Troubled headed straight for her. The kind she might not be able to come back from. But Levi was the first person who had given her a moment of reprieve from the tragedies in her life. For this brief time, she was Skyla from before. If she remembered too much of what it was to be a strong, confident woman again and then it all fell to pieces, she would not survive this time. No amount of making light of her situation would save her.

"It's warmer in here," he said.

Her fingers toyed with her necklace. He had taken the blankets, after all. She didn't want to sleep on the floor without some covering. She could keep an eye on him if he became sicker during the night, but he seemed to be through the worst of it.

Stay or go?

"Skyla, you coming?"

Go. Definitely go.

Chapter Ten

"Bailey Russo is my brother's wife's sister. I may not be the best reference for you. I should've thought about that last night, but I wasn't exactly myself." Levi handed her a cup of coffee.

They stood in the kitchen with the sun coming up over the river, dancing its pink glow across the water. The mug was hot in her hands, chasing away the chill brought on by nerves.

His fever had broken during the night. This morning the color had returned to his cheeks. A brightness had returned to his eyes too. She was glad he felt better but hearing that Bailey was practically related to him presented a problem for both of them.

"You are the best reference because I don't have any other options."

He arched a brow.

"No offense. I'm sure you're a great reference in

different circumstances. But you are literally one of the only people I know at the moment."

"Don't you have an old boss or someone you could call?"

"Did you forget the part where I don't have a job? I wasn't exactly let go with a glowing review."

"You're not one of those nurses that kill their patients, are you?" The laughter on the end of his sentence lightened the weight of what he had said.

"You lived through the night, didn't you?" She had never hurt a single patient. She had been a good nurse, maybe even great at times. But after she lost Emory, she couldn't function anymore. Breathing required a strength she hadn't had. Swaddling a newborn with their tiny fingers and toes to hand to a new mother beaming with unfathomable joy had broken Skyla into pieces that could never be put back together. Every new birth was another knife in an infected wound that wouldn't heal. Her boss at the hospital had no other choice but to let her go.

"They're also going to wonder how we know each other."

"Can't tell the truth about how we met." Last night, she had climbed onto that air mattress next to Levi. He had stretched out on his back but had left plenty of room for her and the blanket turned down, waiting for her. She had turned on her side with her back to him, giving herself some distance. She had been afraid to accidentally touch him. He had only bid her good night before his soft snores filled the room.

When her eyes had popped open and the room was flooded with morning light, he was already out of bed. The blankets had still smelled like him, and she had hunkered under them for a few extra minutes before joining him in the kitchen.

"We could say you are my assistant. I have one of those. Well, had."

"Had?"

"I closed up my business before I came here." He shrugged as if closing a business or even having a business was no big deal.

"Why?"

"Long story."

He didn't share much but had wanted her to spill her story. She would have to make sure he opened up to her too. It was only fair.

"So, I'm your assistant. Why would I follow you here? What kind of assistant am I?"

"Whatever kind you want to be." He gave her a devilish grin.

"That's tempting, but no thanks." She couldn't meet his gaze. Flirting had never been something she was good at and a man like Levi would have never been interested in her. He was probably only teasing her and would never act on something crazy like having feelings for a homeless woman.

"It's the bald head. Isn't it? I can grow my hair back."

"It's not your bald head." She liked the way he looked but hesitated to say as much.

"You don't like guys?"

"I like guys plenty. You aren't used to a woman brushing you off, are you? Not even those of us with nothing to offer except maybe skin lice."

"You don't have skin lice."

"No, I don't. But I also don't have anything to offer someone like you. What do I say when Bailey asks how I came to work for you? Or her boyfriend. He's the one with all the questions. She was ready to hire me on the spot." Skyla needed to drive the conversation away from any innuendo. Levi was probably lonely out here where his brother didn't want him. He must not have a woman tucked away in any corner of the world or he would've at least mentioned her in passing. Mentioned someone. Though he was tight-lipped. Maybe he had women in every state, and he needed one in New Jersey, and she was available.

He regarded her for a moment. His gaze floated around the room before landing back on her. "You can stick to the truth as much as you want. You needed a job. I hired you. You don't have any family keeping you stuck. You wanted to see the Jersey Shore."

"I guess that could work."

"I could just pay you more to work here. You don't have to work there too."

"I want to work there. You're paying me too much as it is."

Levi had thrown out a number for the work she would do. She would clean the whole house, help set up the furniture, do whatever she could in the yard for this time of year, and then try and tackle that tiny shed in the back. He had a vision.

She had tried to argue that he was paying too much since he had also given her a place to live, but she couldn't pick her mouth up off the floor after he announced the amount. She hadn't made anything close to that since she had a full-time nursing job. With Levi's money, she would be able to buy food and maybe some necessities for a while. Longer than she had in months. The idea of not being hungry...

She could use the payment for rent, but she didn't completely trust that either job would last long enough to coincide with a lease. No landlord would rent to her anyway without a job.

"Why do you want to work at the bookstore so much?"

"I don't know. I liked Bailey right away. I guess. She seemed like she needed help through the holidays. I love books. It might be temporary until her employee comes back. Why does it matter?" She couldn't explain the truth to him. He didn't understand what life was like for her even if he was being generous to a fault. She still was suspicious of his kindness. Maybe it was sex he was after in the end. Right now, she didn't know.

"I was curious. You don't have to get angry." He plunked the mug on the counter. The coffee sloshed around inside it.

"I'm not angry. But I don't know why you have to grill me. If you don't want to be a reference, just say it." Her voice shook and she couldn't stop it.

Levi backed up. "Whoa. What's with the outburst?"

"You know what? Never mind. I'll tell Bailey I can't do it. I don't want to owe you any more than I already do. And I'm not going to sleep with you." She whipped around to get out of there before she burned to death from shame.

She grabbed her backpack and her coat, but before she could get her arms inside it, he was standing beside her.

"Don't run away like that."

"I have nothing to say to you." She couldn't meet his gaze.

"You have something to say. You're upset."

"I'll be out of your hair, okay? Just let me pass."

"No. Not okay. What's going on here? I don't understand."

"What's going on? You're some guy who found me squatting in your house and you've gone ahead and dumped a place to live and life-changing money in my lap. You have to want something for it. And whatever that is I won't give it to you. I'll figure myself out. I don't need you." Traitorous tears burned her eyes. She blinked them away and forced her gaze out the front window.

"I'm sorry you've had a hard life. I really am, but I'm not after anything and it sure as hell isn't sex. I don't need to pay for a woman to sleep with me. I've had plenty of willing women in my bed for free."

She didn't know what to say to that. "I didn't mean to imply—"

"Sure, you did. I've been flirting with you because I think you're beautiful. Your hair drives me crazy. But you're also funny and witty and you haven't let life totally ruin you for all your problems as far as I can tell. I'm pretty good at reading people. Had to be. But I'm not looking to buy you for an hour."

"I'm sorry." Guilt pressed against her chest. He thought she was pretty. When was the last time a man looked at her with longing? Ever? She had not been the woman men sought with vigor. She had known those women, worked with those women. Envied those women. She had only wanted the kind of love that stability could stand on.

"I've been accused plenty of being a selfish prick. After my cancer, I decided I would change that about myself. I have a second chance now. The Universe or God or whoever dumped you in my lap. I figured I'd answer the message and help you. But if you want to bite off your nose... go right ahead. This house might suck, but I won't be sleeping in my car tonight." He threw his hand in the air and turned on his heel.

He had only wanted to be nice to her. She couldn't tell the difference any longer. Maybe she never could. She had thought Will loved her, wanted to spend his whole life with her, but he had run when life became too much to handle. She hadn't known Will was that kind of man until she was standing alone in her apartment among the tattered shreds of her life.

"Levi, wait."

He stopped but didn't face her.

"I'm sorry. I don't know how to do this. I don't know how to accept help. Nothing in my life has worked out. It's hard to believe you will."

He turned. "I understand. I used to think nothing would work out for me too until the right person heard my brother sing into a microphone. It only takes one person, one second for everything to change."

"I know about life changing in a minute. But not for the better."

"Do you want to work at the bookstore?"

"I do."

"Give Bailey my number. I'll vouch for you. I'll tell her you're my assistant and that you're a good worker, but you suck at pulling weeds." He winked.

Her smile wobbled on her face, but the breath returned to her lungs. "Thank you."

"No thanks needed. I do have a favor to ask."

"Anything."

"You might not agree when you hear what it is, but I hope you will." He leaned against the molding in bad need of paint and crossed his ankles.

"I doubt you could say anything I wouldn't want to hear."

"I want you to come with me to spread ashes."

"What?" She wasn't expecting that.

"Spread ashes with me. I don't want to go alone." He ducked his head and gave her a tender smile.

"I can't do that." Her fingers pulled at her necklace.

"Why not?" His gaze snapped up.

His ask shook her to the core. She didn't know if she could stand beside him while he set someone free. After Emory, she couldn't go to funerals or hold the hands of anyone who had suffered a loss without breaking down. She would certainly fall apart while he honored someone he must have cared deeply about. That task wasn't for her.

"You have to find someone else. I'm sorry."

He narrowed his eyes. "I don't have anyone else in town, and this is something I've taken too long to take care of. Never mind. I understand." He went into the kitchen.

111

The skin on her hands was dry and cracked. She had cut herself in a couple of places when she had pulled out the weeds. Just nicks. She hadn't even noticed until now.

She owed Levi. If she pretended they were doing something else, she could get through it. She could close her eyes and not look.

She stood in the kitchen. Levi poured another cup of coffee.

"I'll go."

He gave her a sideways glance. "You sure?"

"Sure. I'm sorry. It's just I'm not very good with death."

"No one is. Thank you for agreeing. It means a lot. I'd like to go tomorrow. The day is important. I can meet you at the beach after you're done at the store. Say around noon?"

"I'll be there."

Chapter Eleven

"You work for Levi Hawkins?" Bailey stared at the piece of paper Skyla had written Levi's number on, then back at her. Bailey's eyebrows sank together. She nibbled on her bottom lip.

Skyla held her breath. This was a make-or-break moment. If Bailey turned her away, she could go quietly. Or she could tell her secret. If she lost this job because of her connection to Levi, then maybe she could win it back because of her connection to Bailey.

"It's a new thing." They hadn't discussed how long she had been pretend employed by Levi. They couldn't say it had been a few days. Whatever she came up with, she would have to remember and tell Levi to go along with it.

"This might be a problem." Bailey played with her bracelets.

"Why? I thought we were all set as long as I brought references." Since she had put this lie in motion, she needed to see it to the end. Once Bailey realized what an asset Skyla was around here, she wouldn't regret hiring Skyla.

Two women entered the store on a string of cackles. They each held a to-go cup of coffee. Bailey gave the slightest of head shakes. She either wanted that coffee business or wanted those women to sound less like hens running from a fox.

"Good morning, ladies. Let me know if I can help you find anything."

The two women said they would but headed for the romance section without another word to Bailey.

Bailey turned back to her. "When Jack had asked for references, I couldn't have suspected Levi Hawkins would be it. That's a crazy coincidence."

"Why? Because you know Levi? It's a small world. We're all bumping into each other at one time or another."

"Actually, the problem is that Levi is my brother-in-law's brother, and they don't get along. I don't know how my sister will feel if Levi is coming around."

How would this sister feel when she found she was related to a homeless woman who lied to get a job? Skyla wouldn't be telling her until she came clean with Bailey.

"No one said he'd be here in the bookstore while I worked. And honestly, Bailey, if he's a resident in Serenity, would you really stop him from purchasing books or tea and coffee? He and his brother may have problems, but Levi's money is just as green as the next person's."

Bailey tugged on her bracelets again. Skyla could almost see the wheels turning behind Bailey's eyes. If Skyla knew anything, it was the importance of money and how fast the cash could disappear. Bailey was a smart woman. A bookstore this size turning business away was nothing short of a stupid move.

"That's true. I wouldn't turn his business away. Jack certainly wouldn't and at the end of the day, this is Jack's store. I can't allow my sister's personal problems to interfere with business."

"Then do we have a deal?" A drop of sweat rolled down her spine. The pressure of the situation turned up a notch. Just a few weeks. That was all she needed for Bailey to get to know her and for Skyla to decide what to do with this family secret.

"When did Levi get to town? Kassidy hadn't mentioned he was back."

This woman was like a dog with a peanut butter treat. Skyla would have to ask exactly what went down between him and his brother to have this woman concerned about a connection to him.

"We arrived recently."

"So, you weren't visiting with friends like you had said the other day?"

"I was doing that too. Killing two birds and all that." She had forgotten about that tall tale she had shared. She would have to remember to write down the lies so as not to mix them up. This whole thing was going to be harder than she thought. Taking this job might be a bad idea.

"I just don't know, Skyla."

"Whatever is going on between Levi and his brother is between them. It has nothing to do with my working relationship with him. I'm sure no matter what you might say about Levi, you have to admit he has a good work ethic and knows talent when he sees it." She was going out on a limb with that one. She could assume Levi worked hard. He appeared to have money at his disposal. He did something with the music industry. He had to come across talent and he had praised his brother's voice.

"He is very successful, but he hasn't always been honest on his way there. Honesty is important to my family. We've had enough secrets between us. We don't want any more lies or untruths. Can you understand that?"

"Of course I can. Lies hurt people. But Levi isn't lying about me. Give me a chance. You'll see I'm worth it." Only Levi *was* lying. She didn't want to get Levi into more trouble with his brother, but she needed to work here at least for a little while. As long as no one found out what they were up to, everything would work out.

Bailey glanced at the paper still in her hand. "Okay, I'll trust that he's a credible reference. He is smart, runs a business. And I have a good vibe about you. I feel like we're connected somehow. Like from another life or something."

Or something. "Thanks. You won't regret hiring me."

The door swung open on a swish. The smell of burnt cedar followed a thin man with lanky arms and legs into the store. He wore his hair parted at the side and combed over. He couldn't be more than early thirties. He pushed a pair of broken glasses up his nose. He wore a flannel coat and scuffed boots. Someone Skyla would not give a second glance to if she walked past him.

He smiled when he saw Bailey, revealing crooked teeth.

"Hi." He waved. The tips of his cheeks were pink. Either from the cold or from embarrassment.

"Hi, Colin. Can I help you find anything today?"

"I'm just browsing. A few last-minute Christmas gifts." He turned down the history aisle, out of sight.

The two women who had entered earlier left without buying. They looked in the direction Colin had gone. One of them pointed. Skyla couldn't be sure, but she might have heard one of the women say arsonist.

"Damn. I needed that sale," Bailey said more to herself.

The door opened again and this time a woman with dark hair that waved past her shoulders and a strong jaw entered. She brought the brisk morning air with her and a burst of sunshine.

Bailey's face lit up. "Maren." She ran to the woman and threw her arms around her, almost knocking Maren off-balance.

"Good morning to you too." Maren gripped Bailey's shoulders and righted herself. "I wish everyone greeted me that way."

Bailey's laugh decorated the room like tinsel. "Did you come to help next door?"

"I did. I wanted to see you. But you have a customer. Go help her." Maren pushed Bailey in Skyla's direction.

"Oh, no. This is Skyla Morgan. I've hired her to replace Amy through the holidays. Skyla, this is my oldest sister, Maren."

"Not old. Just the firstborn. Nice to meet you." Maren smiled, but the light didn't reach her eyes. Her gaze took stock of Skyla standing there.

Skyla had worn her best jeans, but they were wrinkled. Her boots were old, and the fake leather was worn through in patches. She had used a permanent black marker to try and fill in the gaps of color. Her coat was also worn near the zipper and had stains she could not get out if her life depended on it. She never wore makeup because she couldn't afford that luxury. She probably had dark circles under her eyes since she and Levi had been up most of the night talking and her lips were chapped.

Skyla could guess what Maren was thinking. That Skyla was either very poor or the wrong kind of person to be working here.

Her voice failed her. She had to swallow to try again. "Nice to meet you too." And it was. She stood before her oldest sister too, hoping her nerves didn't give her away.

"Skyla, can you take some hours tomorrow?"

"Absolutely. I'll just need to know when because I'm still working for Levi too."

"Levi?" Maren said.

"She works for Levi Hawkins." Bailey answered for her.

"You do?" Maren turned to Bailey. "Does Jack know?"

"Not yet, but it's fine. Levi isn't going to be hanging out here."

"If I may jump in, Levi is a good man. I don't know what the problem is between him and his brother and it's none of my business, but you two should know Levi really helped me when I needed it. He gave me a job when no one else would. That has to count for something." Levi had said to stick to the truth as much as possible. Now she had. She had also tipped her hand a little by saying she had needed a job, and no one wanted her.

"I'm not saying that Levi hasn't done some good in his life, but he hurt our sister, Kassidy." Maren's icy stare held hers. "That's not okay in our book. The three of us stick together no matter what because all we have is each other. I shouldn't gossip, but Levi did something to Grant too. I just don't know what that is."

Maren would be a problem. If and when Skyla revealed she was their half sister, her bet was on Maren who would react the worst.

"Like I said, all of that is none of my business. I'm here for a job. Bailey, if my working here makes you uncomfortable because of my connection to Levi, then I'll pull my request." She fought to keep her chin up and her lip from trembling.

She headed for the door, refusing to look back. She had to make it seem as if she didn't need or want this job, that it was their loss. If Bailey wanted her, she would have to figure out how to stand up to the people in her life like Maren and Jack.

The sidewalk was only steps away. Her hand would clasp around the ornate metal doorknob, and she would be gone.

"Skyla, wait."

She turned and collided into a customer. She bounced off Colin's body and tumbled into a display of ornamental Christmas presents. Colin's glasses went askew on his face. The empty boxes fell over and the floor rose up to smack into her knees. Her pride broke in a hundred places.

"I'm sorry." Colin gripped her elbow and hoisted her to her feet. "I didn't see you there."

Shame burned her cheeks. "It's okay."

"Are you two all right?" Bailey hurried toward them.

"Fine," she said. She was anything but. On her big exit, this geeky young man clobbered her and ruined any kind of impactful scene end.

Colin nodded and ran from the store. The door slammed shut on his departure. Looked as though he was allowed the dramatic chapter end instead of her.

"Why did he run off like that?" She was the one who could have injured something. How would she have paid for that? She stared off in the direction Colin had fled.

"He's socially awkward," Bailey said.

"And probably embarrassed," Maren said from her spot at the top of the store.

"I'm sorry about what just happened. Colin is harmless, really. He's a sweet guy with some issues."

She could relate to that. "I understand. He didn't mean anything. I was just startled."

Bailey gave her a wide smile. "Can you work tomorrow?"

She handed Bailey one of the gift boxes. "I'll be here around ten. Thank you." She risked a look at Maren.

Maybe she imagined it, but Maren's head gave the slightest of shakes as she turned away and became busy with the lint on her pants.

Chapter Twelve

Levi waited for Skyla at the boardwalk entrance. She was late. They had said goodbye this morning when she had left for another day of work at the bookstore. She had promised to be here, but she still seemed uncomfortable with the idea.

He was too. But this had to be done, and he had waited way too many years to see it through. Since his brush with death, he was tying up all loose ends. Taking care of what he had ignored before. If forgiveness was something a person in the afterlife, if there was such a thing, offered, he hoped Emmett would offer forgiveness to him.

Gray clouds had rolled in on a strong wind, blocking the sun and what little warmth it provided. He hunkered down in his coat and pressed his knit cap further down on his head. He was about to give up and head to the jetty when Skyla appeared on the street hurrying toward him.

Her red hair hung in those long waves he liked. Her coat was older and about as tired as he was these days, but he didn't care about the disarray of her clothes or the fact she lived in her car. He could replace those things for her.

Her spirit and determination not to let life get her down was the thing that attracted him. He wanted to be under her light because he had been in the darkness for too long.

Yesterday when she came back from the bookstore, he had asked her how things went with Bailey.

"Well, in the end fine," she had said.

"She didn't want to hire you because of me."

"I told her what an upstanding human you are. Then I walked out."

"You walked out?"

"Almost. I wanted her to think I didn't want the job if she was against you. I had made it all the way to the door when a customer accidentally banged into me, dropping me to the floor."

He admired her gumption. His momma had a lot of that while she was alive. Life had been hard for his mother too, and she had done her best to make the most of it for her and her three boys.

Now, Skyla smiled and waved when she noticed him standing on the boardwalk. He wasn't cold any longer. He gave himself a reminder to calm his jets. Theirs was a working relationship. He might have more money than she did, but he hadn't been a good partner in his past relationships. Skyla didn't deserve to get caught up in his mess.

"I'm sorry I'm late." She stood before him breathless. Her cheeks were dotted pink and her green eyes lit up.

"How was work today?"

"I only screwed up the register three times. Jack doesn't

have a lot of patience, but Bailey is fantastic. I wish I had her energy. Maren, on the other hand, is a real pill. She's helping with the design of the new space and she's going to be there all the time. She definitely doesn't like me."

"Maren is very protective of the other two and doesn't like me either. I don't even think she liked Grant at first. Steer clear of her, if you can." He wanted to reach for her but didn't risk it. Ironic, he had been a pretty good risk-taker once.

"I'll try. So, do you want to walk down to the ocean?"

"Walk with me onto the jetty."

"The jetty? Oh, I don't know. They're slippery. The rocks are jagged, and the water is cold if we get hit by the spray. Can I just stand on the sand?"

"You've never been on a jetty before, have you?"

"No. I don't think it's for me."

"I'll keep you safe." He meant that and held out his hand. If she didn't take it, he would leave her up here on the boardwalk. He had wanted company for what he was about to do. He wasn't looking to upset her.

She slid her hand in his and followed him. Her thin fingers were cold, and he blew on them to warm her some. She smiled up at him, a half smile as if a full one might cost too much and something in his chest shifted. He could picture her naked with that long hair draped over her breasts as she lay under him. He stopped.

"Why did you stop?"

He wanted to know everything about her. Who was the first man she loved, what did she dream about, what was she most afraid of?

"Have you ever been married?" He continued his journey to the jetty.

"I was for a while. We divorced a few years back. What about you?"

"Never married. I liked playing the field."

"How did that work out for you?"

"Not the way I thought." He hadn't wanted to be tied down when the music world was good to him. Every new town and city had women screaming for the band. Whatever woman couldn't get their hooks into Grant, because he was the star, were happy to settle for Grant's younger brother. Levi had played in the band for a while but then switched to Grant's manager after Grant didn't want to play any longer. Becoming Grant's manager had opened a new door for Levi. Other musicians wanted him to help them hit stardom. And he had done it. But he was never happy in that role. He had wanted back on stage. That was one reason why he had lied to Grant.

"Life rarely works out the way we think," she said.

Black rocks that made up the jetty extended from the beach out into the ocean. The top of the jetty was flat as if some engineer had poured cement over the rocks to hold them together and maybe someone had. Jetties helped slow down beach erosion and the rocks were placed on the Jersey beaches by a human and not a force of nature like on the West Coast.

He wanted to be farther out on the jetty away from the sand to empty Emmett's ashes into the sea. The jetty narrowed at that end and those rocks were slick with wet moss.

"I'll climb up and then help you." The rocks on the side of the jetty, the uneven and jagged ones, they'd need to climb would be the most difficult to navigate for her.

"These ashes that you're spreading, you can't do it somewhere else? Maybe off the end of a pier?"

A wave crashed against the rocks, spraying its white foam everywhere.

"I have to do it this way." He hopped up with ease. He'd been climbing and hiking his whole life. He moved fine after the surgery. His problem was in his head now. Not in his pants.

"Don't let me fall." She gripped his hand like a vise.

He didn't want to let on that she was crushing his fingers. She might let go and scramble away and end up slipping.

"I've got you." He gave a gentle tug, and she found her footing. When she got almost to the top, she slipped and let out a scream. He yanked her toward him without thinking. She banged into his chest. He wrapped an arm around her waist and held her close.

He looked into her eyes and fear stared back. She was small against him, fragile like the shells under their feet. He didn't know her full story, the pain she had experienced, but he wanted to protect her from any more hurt. He wanted to keep her close, away from the unforgivable storms and the cold biting wind. He had only known her days, but the connection went deeper.

"Thank you." The ocean's roar took her voice away, but he could read her lips.

She stayed against him, shivering.

"If you want to go back, you can." He couldn't allow her to be here as some payment to him. He could do this alone. He hadn't wanted to, but he wanted her to be frightened far less.

"I want to stay."

"I'm going to have to let you go to get something out of my pocket." The last thing he wanted was to release her. She fit against him.

She gave a crisp nod and stepped to the side.

He fished out the small jar from his inside jacket pocket and moved down the jetty, stopping to make sure she was behind him. Each step brought them farther out into the ocean. If they fell in here, they would be crushed against the rocks by the waves.

She gripped his arm. "Levi, what are you doing?"

"I need to be over the water."

"I don't understand. Just pour them out here. The wind will take them." Tears filled her eyes, but it could be from the wind.

"Okay. I won't go any farther. I'll tell you everything when we're done. This will only take a minute." It took him two tries to unscrew the lid with his frozen fingers. He put the lid in his coat pocket.

He slid his hand into Skyla's. She shivered beside him but gave his hand a squeeze. With his other hand, he set Emmett's ashes free. The wind picked them up and carried them out to sea.

Waves crashed against the rocks in a thick white arc of frothy lather as if the swells also reached for Emmett.

Levi closed his eyes and let the memories wash over

him. Emmett smiling. Emmett playing music. Emmett yelling as the bus turned over.

Skyla gripped his hand harder. He opened his eyes.

She pointed.

To Grant standing on the sand.

Levi wanted to close his eyes again. He turned to Skyla. "I'll help you down, but then you should go back to the house or wherever your plans for today were going to take you. I need to talk to my brother."

"I can wait up on the boardwalk."

"It's cold out. You'd be better off inside." He didn't want her to witness the argument that was about to ensue. For now, she liked him, and he wanted to keep it that way for as long as possible. If she heard him argue with Grant, she would change her mind as fast as the tide.

"I don't mind the cold. I can wait."

"At least wait in the bakery with a cup of coffee."

She looked away. He wanted to smack his head for the ignorant thing he just said. He dug cash out of the front pocket of his jeans and gave it to her. It was more than he'd said he'd give her for the week, but he didn't care. He didn't want the money.

"Here. It's this week's pay," he said.

"I'm not going to count it, but it feels like too much. And I won't argue because your brother could kill with that look. Go talk to him."

Levi helped Skyla down and they stood before Grant.

"Grant, this is Skyla Morgan. Skyla, my brother, Grant Hawkins."

"Ma'am," Grant said with a curt nod and a cold stare.

Levi wanted to shake his brother for making it obvious to Skyla he didn't want to talk to her.

But Skyla returned with a warm hello. Her smile wavered, but only for a second before she righted it again.

"Levi, I'll meet you in the bakery." She hurried off without waiting for a response.

He watched her until she climbed the stairs to the boardwalk before turning to Grant.

"What were you doing up on the jetty?" Grant spat the words.

He could make up a lie. He'd already withheld the truth about his illness. He had lied to his brother a few times in their lives. What was one more? But he didn't want to lie. He wanted this new season of his life to be honest. With his second chance, he wanted to do better.

He held Grant's gaze and braced himself for what was to come. "Spreading some of Emmett's ashes."

"Out here? Why?" Grant's gaze swiveled around the jetty and the ocean as if the answer to his question was out to sea.

"Because he told me once he wanted his ashes dumped in the ocean. The jetty was as close as I could get." He and Emmett had been up late the night their stepfather had died. Grant had given up on them and gone to bed. He and Emmett had sat on the back patio of their double-wide trailer, smoking cigars. They had talked about their lives as children and how much they hated their stepfather. The funeral would be the next day and neither of them had thought anyone would show.

"Cremate me," Emmett had said, staring at the night sky.

"Shut up. You're not gonna die."

"Someday, brother. We're all gonna die. If I go first, find the biggest ocean you can and drop me in it."

"The biggest ocean is the Pacific, you numbnuts."

"You know what I mean. Any ocean. Just do it."

"Whatever, Emmett." Little did he know Emmett would be gone way before his time and Levi would be standing on the Jersey Shore doing exactly what his brother had asked.

"He never said that." Grant's words yanked him back to the present moment like a hairpin turn on two wheels.

"He did say it."

"Why'd you wait till now to take care of things? He's been gone for years."

Over five to be exact. "Now seemed like a good time. I'm living in this town. It has an ocean."

"I can't believe you moved into my town and dumped our brother's ashes without telling me. I don't understand you."

"Why did you walk down here?" He would have to push Grant until he broke. His brother was the most stubborn person on the planet. Levi had to make up a story three years ago just to get Grant to meet him in Serenity by the Sea. Levi had needed him to finish writing songs for the record label about to sue them. He couldn't think of another way to make Grant write those songs except lie to him before they had lost everything.

"I saw you up there pouring dust in the wind."

"And you wanted to see if I had Emmett's ashes."

"You had no right to scatter Emmett like that." Grant kicked the sand.

"You have your own portion. Do what you want with it." They had divided up the ashes after the funeral home had returned them. Levi hadn't wanted them, but Grant had forced him and now he was grateful. He was able to give his brother his last request even if Emmett hadn't known it was.

"Him."

"What?"

"You said do what I want with it. Emmett is no it."

"It ain't him, Grant. Emmett's gone." He had accepted that fact sooner than Grant. It had taken Grant years to shake the guilt of that night.

"Those ashes are all we have left. How can you dump them?" Grant said.

"I wanted him to have his last wish."

"He never told me he wanted that." Grant looked out over the ocean again.

He wished for his brother's sake that Emmett would come up out of the water and tell him everything was all right.

"You know Emmett, he wasn't going to tell you because he'd know you'd go and make the plans then and there. You were always taking care of us."

"Still..."

"He said it the first time when Tony died. Then he said it again when Philip Diamond OD'd. He was worried the same might happen to him, so he let me know what to do if it did."

The wind howled against the sea. He was ready to get off the beach and go find Skyla at the bakery. The cold stole the feelings from his fingers and toes and seeped deep into his bones. The aches and pains would start up soon and he wanted to be somewhere warm when they did.

"Why didn't you ask me to come? You let some woman working for you stand by while you said goodbye to Emmett."

"I said goodbye to Emmett a long time ago. I couldn't ask you. You wouldn't have come, and I didn't want to do this alone."

"Since when do you ever want company?"

Since the cancer, but he didn't say that. "Come to the bakery with me. Meet Skyla. You'll like her. We can talk."

"About what?"

"About nothing or everything. I don't care. I just want to talk to you."

"Nothing to talk about. What's done is done. You lied to me. Twice." He turned and marched away.

"Grant, wait." But his words died in the wind.

Chapter Thirteen

Skyla walked past the bakery. She couldn't sit still right now and had no way of knowing how long Levi and Grant would be. Grant was the opposite appearance of Levi. Stockier. More lines on his face as if he'd lived a hard life outdoors. He had worn faded jeans and cowboy boots, seemed like a dumb idea on the sand, but then who was she to judge. Instead of a winter coat, he had sported only a plaid flannel jacket.

She wanted Levi to take all the time he needed if he could fix things between him and Grant, but she couldn't wait for him at the bakery and sent a text.

Skipping bakery. See you at house.

She turned off her phone, avoiding his response. He might tell her to wait or that he understood. Either reply was too much to handle at the moment. His kindness or his disappointment would only carve into the hole in her heart.

Leaving Levi at the beach would buy her a little time. Her insides had come unglued while he stood on that jetty and not because she had been terrified she would slip and fall, cracking her head on the rocks.

Her feet slapped the cold sidewalk as she worked her way back up Main Street to where she parked her car. She slid in behind the wheel and started the engine. Even with the heat turned up on high, she still shivered. She needed to get out of there and didn't know where to go.

Levi's house seemed like the only place. She could walk along the river. No one would be out there. Or she could tear up more of the yard. She needed to earn her keep and calm her mind. Two birds and all that.

His brother's ashes. When Levi had turned that jar upside down, she wanted to scream for him to stop, don't let the wind take him, but she swallowed the words like poison and had been surprised when the poison hadn't killed her.

After Emory... her brain hurt to think about it, but she had to remember. She owed it to Emory. After Emory, Skyla could not bear the idea of what lay ahead during the funeral services.

She had wanted to give Emory her favorite blanket because she was alone and might get cold. Will had stopped her from placing the blanket inside the coffin. Skyla had wanted to pick out Emory's favorite outfit. The pink and purple sweatshirt where the colors swirled together like fingerpaints and the matching pants. Will had taken the clothes when she wasn't looking and disposed of them.

Skyla could not function in those days. She could not eat or sleep. She could not sit still or walk. She had become a zombie, existing, and wanted nothing more than to stop the pain. Will had taken over the arrangements while she stared out the window, wondering if Emory was in the breeze playing with the leaves.

She had been grateful for Will in those early days. He had stepped up, wearing his pain like a long wool coat in ninety-degree heat, and took charge. He was good at taking charge. He answered the questions, made the payments, and allowed her to crumble in on herself. Yes, she had been grateful, until she found out what he had done.

He had turned their little girl to ash. He had packed up her clothes and her blankets and her stuffed animals and placed them in cardboard boxes he had left by the apartment dumpster to be scavenged by anyone with greasy hands or dirty minds.

What good were they, he had said. Emory couldn't use them anymore. Will had walked out the next day, leaving Skyla alone to drown. She had climbed into that dumpster, but it was too late. Emory's things were gone. All that Skyla had left was the necklace. A memorial necklace with a little bit of Emory near her heart every day.

Today, with Levi, how simple it had seemed for him to turn that jar upside down. As if it didn't cost him anything. Of course, it wasn't his child. Those ashes belonged to his brother. She didn't know the whole story. She only knew hers. Her hurt. Her pain. Her suffering. All of which had led her to living in her car, desperate for a family to fill the giant black hole in her chest.

Christmas decorations on the front lawns she sped past took on a grotesque quality. Their colors had grayed like the sky. Their shapes had warped and melted. They haunted her. Reminded her of what she didn't have.

She turned onto River Road and flew down the street, screeching her way into the drive. Hopping from the car, she gulped the cold air to calm her heart which did not work.

The river called to her. The surface was flat like dark glass since there was no sun to brighten up the water. The old dock swayed on its last leg. If it had been in good shape, she might run off its end and into the water. She can't swim. Had never learned. She would allow her heavy coat to pull her under. Life had no point to it.

All this trying to come back from the worst possible thing did not let go of the grip on her like a weight tied to her ankle. Finding Bailey would not change anything. Working anywhere would not change anything. She would be as alone as she was in that moment.

She walked to the yard's edge where the ground crumbled away under her feet and into the water. It was a straight drop. Not far, but she couldn't see below the surface to what lay beneath. More rocks maybe. Something she could fall on. She stood on her toes. A good wind could push her in. She'd never feel pain again...

"Young lady, what are you doing?"

She whipped around at the barking sound of a man's voice coated with many years of use. Her foot slipped and her arms windmilled. She flung herself onto the grass before she could drop into the water.

This old man with sprigs of white hair flapping in the wind came toward her at remarkable speed for someone with a hitch to his gait. He pumped his fists like a side rod on a steam locomotive.

She pushed to stand.

"Were you about to jump in that water?" He stopped inches from her, his breath coming in short spurts.

"I..." She turned toward the water, then back to him. "No. Is that what you thought?"

"It's sure what it looked like. Do you live here?"

"Who are you?"

"Me? Name's Melvin Trubador. I've lived in that house right there since the sixties." He pointed to the first house on the street. "I've never seen you before today."

"I'm a friend of Levi's. He just bought this house." She hitched her thumb over her shoulder to take away any confusion.

"I met that young man. Nice enough. Said he's going to fix the place up. We'll see. Young people are lazy these days. Not like in my time."

"Is there something I can help you with?"

"Not me. I was trying to help you. Looked like you were about to take a plunge in that cold water with all your clothes on. Not exactly a leisurely swim, I'd say."

"I appreciate your concern, but it is unwarranted. I was looking down and only slipped when you screamed at me."

"I had to stop you. Like laying on the car horn, is all."

"You stopped me from nothing. You did scare me, though."

"Sorry about the scare. I'll get back to my place." He turned to go but turned back. "You smell that?"

She took a deep inhale. "Woodsmoke?"

"Might be, but we're kind of far from anyone's house and I didn't light a fire today. Did you?"

"Nope."

"It's that person who is setting the trees on fire."

"The Christmas trees?"

"That's the one."

"Why is he doing that?" Or she. It could be a she.

"Angry. Hurt. Scared maybe. People do a lot of things for reasons only they understand. I just hope whoever it is doesn't come down our street. These homes would go up in seconds."

Levi pulled into the driveway behind Skyla's car. He hadn't noticed before how the paint peeled away around the bumper which hung a little loose on one side. Her back window was full of what looked like junk but was all important stuff to her. He wasn't sure how she could see out the back when she drove.

After he had read her text, he drove around some to shake off the conversation with Grant. On the one hand, Grant had come down to the sand to find out what he was doing which might mean that Levi was getting through to him. On the other, Grant still walked away mad, leaving him alone on the beach. Levi couldn't win, but he would keep trying. Something had to change the way Grant felt about him. What that something could be was anyone's guess.

Branches in various shapes and sizes piled up in the side yard and were abandoned as if waiting to be rescued from their tangled mess. Skyla must have gone around the yard, picking up debris, but she was nowhere to be seen now.

He didn't care if she cleaned the yard or the house. He had only wanted to find a way to help her and offering her the job seemed like the logical choice. She obviously needed the money. If she left those branches there to rot, it would not faze him.

Before he was out of the car, Melvin hurried across the front lawns.

"Hey, Melvin." He grabbed the sandwiches out of the trunk that he bought from the deli. He thought Skyla might like to try them and he was starving. They could have a late lunch, early dinner thing.

"Levi. Do you have a minute? I need to talk to you about something important." Melvin's chest heaved with each breath.

The sun had dropped out of the sky in a hurry and cast long shadows on the ground. The day had run away from him somehow and he was anxious to get inside and light a fire with some of those branches.

"For you, I have the rest of the afternoon." He had liked Melvin from the minute he had met him. The one time Charlotte, the real estate agent, had brought Levi to see the house, Melvin had stood on the front yard demanding to know if Levi was interested in the place. Melvin had told him no one had lived in that house in over ten years, and he was the only resident on this street. What was Levi's intentions because Melvin didn't want some developer coming in and buying up this little piece of land, building big houses on it and pushing Melvin out. Levi respected him instantly.

"I met your friend today." Melvin glanced at the house.

"Skyla?"

"That's her. She raked your yard earlier, as you can see. A lot of fire in that belly of hers. I told her to leave those branches where they were. No point in doing work twice and they weren't bothering anything. Save work like that for spring. The rest of winter is going to come in here and whip more branches into our yards with the park across the street."

"But she didn't listen to you."

"Not a word. Never met a woman who wasn't as stubborn as a goat. She wanted to burn up some energy, she said. But that's not what I wanted to mention."

"Okay. Do you want to come inside and talk about it?"

"Nah. This will be quick. I looked out my kitchen window earlier and I see this woman standing too close to the river's edge with arms out like she might swan dive right into the water."

"Did she?"

"No, of course not. I would've told you that first. Smart guy like you knows not to bury the lead."

"Appreciate that."

"I watched for only a minute. Too risky to wait longer. I sure couldn't figure out why anyone would be out there in all this wind on this cold day, staring at the water like it might be a demon summoning them. I ran outside as fast as these old legs can carry me. Temperatures and current would get her if whatever's under the water didn't."

"Smart move to help her." He would be asking Skyla what she was doing.

"I called out to her three times before she heard me. My legs might not work so good, but my lungs are just fine. When she looked at me, it was like she didn't see me at first."

"But then she did."

"Deep in thought, I guess. But thoughts that might not be good ones."

"Do you think she would've jumped if you hadn't come outside?"

"No way to tell. But if she didn't mean herself no harm and just slipped and fell, those rocks would have cut her up pretty good."

"Did you ask her what she was doing?"

"In so many words. She claimed she was just looking at the water. Meditation or something like that. But her eyes. They gave her away. Empty-like."

"I understand."

"I noticed her car, Levi. She living out of it? Moving?"

"She's in between places at the moment. That's why she's bunking with me."

"You might want to have a word with her anyway. I would hate to see an accident happen that could be avoided."

"Thanks for the information, Melvin, but Skyla is a grown woman. If she wants to talk about her problems, assuming she has any, that's up to her. I can't pry."

"Are you her friend?"

"Yes." And he wanted to be more, he was quickly figuring out.

"If you're her friend, then you'll ask. You'll find a way.

But I don't think it's a good idea for this street to have the reputation of people offing themselves. Others will start showing up."

"I think you might be worrying about nothing. This is all private property."

"Like anyone with a mission to stop their pain is going to care about that."

"I better get inside." He pointed to the deli bag to make his point.

Melvin looked at the sky. "Angry clouds. Storm's coming. Freezing rain."

The clouds hung low, waiting to release what they held. Wind ran through the bare branches of the maples and oaks and shook the pine needles. A cold shudder ran down his back. He glanced toward the park with the sense they weren't alone.

"Another reason to get inside, then. Are you all set if a storm comes through? You need anything?"

"Got everything I need. But you watch yourself in there. Your friend might be trouble."

"Why do you say that?"

"Those Christmas tree fires."

"You think Skyla is behind those?" He tried not to laugh. He'd been with her almost every minute of the last few days. No way she could be lighting trees on fire.

"They started same time she showed up. I've seen things like this before. I used to volunteer for the fire department."

"That's crazy, Melvin. Skyla's not starting those fires."

"Watch yourself anyway. Something's off with that

one." Melvin hurried back across the front lawn of the vacant house.

Levi stood there until Melvin went inside, wondering where that old coot could get an insane idea like Skyla setting fires to trees. She would have a good laugh over that one too.

He turned and found her standing on the front porch. Her hair blew in the wind. A blanket was draped over her shoulders.

"Hey." The excitement that ran through his veins surprised him. He should watch himself, but not because she was the arsonist. Because he was in over his head and way too soon.

"He thinks I'm nuts, doesn't he?"

Chapter Fourteen

Skyla had dragged the mattress out into the living room and against the wall, tired of sitting in the bedroom or on the floor anywhere else. She arranged the few pillows they had to make a futon like setup. She had attempted to start a fire, but with no luck. In time this house would resemble a home, but not today.

Now she stood by as Levi brought a fire to life with expert skills. The flames danced in the wind that swirled down from the open flue.

"Better?"

"Were you a Boy Scout?"

He laughed. "Not at all. I liked to go camping. It gave me an excuse to get away from my stepfather."

She never had a stepfather. Her mother had never married. For most of her life it had been her and her mother. Until Will had come along. He was her first real boyfriend, and they had spent years together before they had married and had Emory. Skyla's mother had cautioned her against

Will time and again. Said she was wasting the best years of her life, but Skyla hadn't listened. Will was everything she wasn't and her chance at a way out of the life she seemed destined to have.

"The flames make it cozy in here," she said.

"The furniture arrives tomorrow. We'll have a sofa, some lamps, a couple of tables, a small kitchen set, and one bed. I didn't know I would have a houseguest." He ran a hand over the top of his smooth head.

"The air mattress is fine with me." It beat the back seat of her car any day and if Levi could keep making her fires, she would be set for a very long time.

"I can order a second one tonight."

"That's not necessary. I don't need much, and we don't even know how long I'll be here."

"You deserve to sleep in a bed."

Tears surprised her. She opened her mouth to thank him, but nothing came out. Instead, she hurried into the kitchen and stared out the window at the river. The surface had turned a steel gray. Opaque. But the wind cut into the water, slicing it into small pieces.

"Are you okay?" Levi had followed her in and stood behind her. He smelled of fresh air and promises.

"Fine." Her pat answer.

"You say you're fine a lot, but I'm not sure I believe you each time. What has you upset? Was it what I said about sleeping in a bed?"

"Someone like you can't understand what it's like to be someone like me."

"What am I like?"

"You're rich. You don't worry about money. You have options."

"Those things are true, but they weren't always. I do understand what it's like to go without food or safety. I also know what it's like to feel as if all your options are gone. Maybe for different reasons, but the feeling is close."

She went back into the living room without answering him. The fire's heat called to her, and she wanted to be near it. Levi joined her on the mattress.

"Tell me what it was like for you growing up," she said.

He undid the laces of his boots, took them off, and put them aside. "Not much to tell. My mom passed when I was young. I have two brothers. The three of us lived with our stepfather until we were old enough to move out. Grant and Emmett are older. They left me first, which was hard being stuck with Tony. That's my stepfather. Was. He's gone now too. Tony used his fists to make his point. Drank his paycheck every week. If I looked hard enough for trouble, I could find it anywhere."

"You're almost glamorizing it."

"If you want the gritty version, ask Grant. He prefers those details. I just want to forget sometimes. Can't go back and change any of it." He lifted a shoulder as if growing up without love and security was no big deal.

"I'm sorry that happened to you."

"Don't be. I learned to think on my feet. I also learned how to talk my way into anything I wanted. It's what made me a good band manager."

"That's what you did?"

"Not at first. At first, I was in the band. But then

Emmett died in a bus accident, and I became the manager. The biggest problem was my only client didn't want to work so I had to go out and get other clients."

"Did you?"

He pulled at a string on the blanket. A hint of a smile crossed his face. "Funny enough, I did. Several. Many. Then I got sick and sold everything. The end." He glanced up at her, his smile wider this time, but it didn't reach his dark eyes.

"It's hard for you to talk about it."

"No point. It's all in the past." He shifted until he sat beside her, their backs pressed against the wall, the fire swaying before them.

"Do you want to talk about getting sick?"

"Nope. What did you think of Melvin?"

Before she became a maternity ward nurse, Skyla had treated many male patients who did not want to discuss their illnesses with anyone. Sometimes not even their doctors. Some men believed a sickness or disease made them weak. She would give Levi the space he wanted. When he was ready, he would tell her more. Or not.

"Melvin seemed like a bit of a nosey neighbor." Melvin's arrival at the river had frightened her. She had been thinking about jumping in when he had appeared out of nowhere to stop her. She never believed that God or the Universe wanted good things for the people walking the earth. She didn't think God heard a thing anyone prayed for, but Melvin's timing had stopped her from doing something rash.

"He's a good guy. He's lived out here for fifty years. His wife died some time back on Thanksgiving. He's lonely."

"He thought I was going to jump into the river." She needed to find out what Levi would think of her frame of mind.

Levi leaned his head against the wall and looked straight ahead instead of at her. "Were you?"

"Is that what you think?"

"Skyla, I'm not accusing you of anything. I want to know if something is bothering you."

"Why don't we have those sandwiches? It was so nice of you to buy them. Thank you." She jumped up and ran back into the kitchen to grab paper plates and napkins.

"You're avoiding me." He had followed her again.

"I'm not. I'm just hungry. We could have a picnic in front of the fire. We didn't get to do that with the soup the other night." She held up two plates and flashed what she hoped was a convincing smile. The droop of his mouth said she had failed at convincing him.

Levi followed her back and sat beside her. He took a bite of his sandwich. "You aren't going to tell me."

He wasn't asking. "Not much to tell. How did it go with Grant after I left? He seemed pretty mad." She wasn't ready to peel off the scab of her story.

"Grant is often mad. He'll come around eventually."

"What happened between you two?"

"If I tell you, will you tell me what upset you today?"

"Nothing upset me."

"Then why were you standing on the edge of the grass

147

almost ready to slip into that river? If you had fallen, you would have either gone into hypothermia or drowned."

"Why do you care?"

"Don't start that thing you do."

"What thing?"

"You get angry and act like I'm the bad guy for caring about you."

"You hardly know me. There's nothing to care about."

"How wrong you are. Haven't you ever been in someone's company and felt an instant attraction to them?"

"No." That was a bald-faced lie. The second she had woken up to find Levi standing above her, every particle in her body came to life. He shone a light down the dark tunnel she had traveled for a long time. She had never experienced a full-body attraction like that around anyone. And every time she was in his company after, that warm, safe light grew brighter. Like now. If she were brave enough, she would push the food aside and kiss him, showing him how big her lie was.

"Well, you're missing out." He shook his head.

"Does this instant attraction thing happen to you all the time?"

"It's only happened once." He held her gaze and her breath stilled.

The fire's crackle was the only sound in the room. The wind picked up outside and slipped between the cracks in the floor, freezing the moment. She wanted to remember this night forever. Levi only inches from her, but out of reach as the flames glowed against his cheek and her longing for him to touch her.

"I'm not good for you." Her words were barely a whisper.

"Let me be the judge of that." His fingers twirled the ends of her hair.

"I have nothing to offer you."

"I don't need things, Skyla. I only want to feel the way I do when I'm around you. I haven't felt this alive in a long time. When I'm with you, I want to live again."

She didn't understand how this was happening. No man had spoken to her this way when she had a job and a home.

"How can that be? How can I mean anything to you at all? If all you're looking for is someone to fix, go find someone else. I'll be okay. I will." She would be too. Her life was taking longer to pull together than she had hoped, but things were working out at the bookstore with Bailey. With a new job, Skyla had a shot.

"I know you'll be just fine. That's why I was surprised when Melvin told me you were standing on the edge of the grass ready to jump. That didn't seem like you."

"You don't know me."

"Then tell me what I don't know. Tell me everything."

The wind shook the house and rattled the thin windows as if to warn her. Once she let the words free, she would never be able to take them back. She would have to sit with Levi's judgment, good or bad. For now, with the words still trapped inside her, she could dream that Levi would love her.

"Why do you want to hear my story?"

"Because I want to kiss you and I'm afraid if I do before

you tell me your story, you're going to get in that old car of yours and run for your life, thinking I can't handle whatever you're going to say. I can. I'm far from perfect. I have a history too."

The decision to tell him bounced from yes to no in her head. Letting out the poison inside her might set her free. She could rid herself of the burden of all the things she did wrong and move forward. Maybe with Levi.

"Do you have children?" She knew little about him. He may have a past, like he said, but she had no idea how his past would stack up against hers.

"No. But I'd like to someday."

She grabbed the blanket, pulled it up to her chin, and settled against the pillows. The sandwich no longer interested her. She set her gaze on the fire and let the flames blur in her vision. Looking at the fire would be easier than watching Levi's face as her story unfolded.

"I do. She was a beautiful little girl with red hair and big green eyes. When she laughed, she'd shove her fists up to her mouth and shake all over. She had chubby little arms. Every time she laughed, I did too. Nothing in this world has sounded so magical. Not the crash of the ocean or the crescendo of a song. Nothing. Emory was my whole world. I didn't know how much I could love one person until she arrived. I had so much love for her, it would spill out of me in my tears, my smile. My heart expanded until I thought for sure it would burst with my love."

She fought the images playing in her head like an old movie. She didn't want to see her child's face light up with delight. The absence of those moments brought the pain from a thousand knives making small, deliberate slices in her skin. The cutting never ended. A dark, rotting hole grew inside her every time she reached back for the times where life was filled with joy. Grief was her archenemy.

"I'm sorry, Skyla." Levi slipped his hand into hers. "You don't have to talk about this if you don't want to. I had no idea."

She kept their hands linked. He was the lifeline holding her above water. "We found out she had acute myeloid leukemia when she was two. My ex-husband and I, that is. Two. What child should have to suffer at that age? At any age? But my Emory was a champion. She barely cried when needles were stuck in her arm. Only her bottom lip would tremble. She would look at me as if to say, why is this happening? And I had no answers. Nothing. Not a one. I tried to tell her it would all be okay. That this would make her feel better. But that was a lie."

She had lied to her child. Eventually the needles only made Emory worse. She would be sick for days, and Skyla would hold her, rubbing her back, singing her songs. Songs that if she heard now would rip her insides into pieces.

They saw more and more doctors. New doctors. Old doctors. And no one had the answers they wanted. That they needed.

She stopped the movie playing in her head at the part that would have her running, like Levi said, but straight into that river. The part where she could not keep her child safe from the demon taking over her ravaged little body.

"Afterward, I couldn't function. I couldn't get out of bed. I didn't want to live without Emory. Will left me. He was right to. He had his own grief; I wasn't there to help him. We should've been there for each other, but I couldn't be there for myself. When I finally returned to work, I couldn't do my job. Patients having babies needed me to take care of them and their children. And all I wanted to do was scream at the top of my lungs at how unfair the world was."

Levi reached over and wiped a tear from her face. His warm touch soothed the blood freezing in her veins. When had she started to cry? When would the tears end?

Levi had tears in his eyes too.

She did it then. She placed a salty kiss on his lips. He kissed her back. A fight to live sparked deep inside her, but she pushed it back down. She had lost all rights to pleasure when she had failed as a mother to take care of her child.

But he cupped the back of her head to take the kiss deeper. She jumped into the kiss as if it were the river outside thrashed by the wind. Anything to forget.

The current swept her away. The old movies playing in her head faded to black and were replaced with the sensation of Levi's mouth claiming hers.

She held him as he eased her back onto the mattress and reminded her that it was okay to live—at least for now.

Chapter Fifteen

Levi made a big mistake. He should not have kissed Skyla back. She was vulnerable, and he didn't want to take advantage of her.

He eased out of the embrace and looked at her beneath him. He brushed her hair from her face. She was a sight he could look at every day.

"You don't have to do this."

"This is my decision. You aren't forcing anything here. I want to feel something other than grief." She placed a cold hand on his cheek.

Now he'd have to tell her the whole truth about his cancer. She didn't need to hear his story after what she had shared. His problems didn't compare to hers, and he wasn't ready for show and tell. Hadn't been with a woman since the surgery. He was less than now. Whole and broken at the same time.

"Well... I'm the one who can't do this." He sat up.

Her eyes widened. She scurried to the corner of the

mattress. He wished he didn't have to say anything, but he did want to spare her more pain and him any embarrassment.

"I understand." She pulled up the blanket to her chin.

"It's not you."

"Please spare me the *it's not you it's me* speech. I hate that one."

"It's not a speech. I shouldn't have kissed you."

Her eyebrows shot into her hairline. He was blundering this.

"I didn't mean it like that. I'm glad we kissed. I truly am. It's me." He'd rather tell her every other humiliating moment in his life before sharing that he didn't look like other men any longer. His doctors had suggested he talk to a therapist about his loss, but he had brushed the idea off like a cold shoulder. He didn't need a therapist. He also hadn't expected to find a woman he wanted in his life so soon after either. Someone like Skyla wasn't supposed to come along for a while, if at all. Love had never been in the cards for him.

"We can just forget it, okay? I'm sorry I kissed you." She swatted at her face.

"Please don't cry." Watching her cry a river broke his heart. She had experienced extraordinary pain and still stood. He would never have been able to get through what she had. He didn't want to be the reason more pain came her way.

She shook her head and squared her shoulders. "I'm fine. See?"

He was a total screwup. He had screwed up everything

in his life. He had ruined his relationship with Grant. He had nearly destroyed Grant's reputation. He had lied to Kassidy. He hadn't been a very good brother to Emmett either. Spreading his ashes had been one way Levi could make amends. That was why he had done it.

"I can go." She pushed off the mattress. The blanket pooled at her feet.

"Don't go. Please." He had to make this right.

"What do you want from me? I just spilled my guts all over the place and then kissed you like an idiot."

He stood too. "You're not an idiot. You were brave for sharing your story. I don't want to cause you any suffering. You've been through enough."

"You don't want to be with me because I lost my child? I don't understand." She threw her arms in the air.

"No. That's not it at all. I admire you for still having the strength to keep going." He wanted to pull her back into his arms, but he didn't.

"Yeah, well, I'm not doing such a bang-up job." She went to the window filled by the last of the day's light and the gray sky. The wind hadn't relented. The storm wasn't far away.

"It's starting to snow," she said, facing the window.

"We're going to get hit pretty hard." He hoped the power held. This house offered nothing except its four walls and some heat.

"Unusual for this time of year." She faced him again.

"Especially at the beach. Might turn out to be an ice storm."

"Levi, I'm going to leave before the storm comes. I'd like

to be somewhere safe. I have enough money to get a hotel room out on the highway." She dipped her head and stared at the floor. "Thanks to you."

He didn't want her to leave. If she could be brave, he should give it a try.

"Kissing you was the best thing that's happened to me in a very long time. I just don't want to cause you any more pain by being with me."

"Why do you keep saying that being with you will cause me pain? What does that mean, Levi?"

"I'm the idiot. Would you sit back down with me?"

She didn't move. He had to be near her and crossed the small room. He tilted her chin so she would have to look at him. "You're not going anywhere."

"What's my reason to stay?"

"Because I want you to."

"What are you holding back?"

"When I tell you, it might change the way you look at me. I don't want that to change." Right in this second, he was still a whole man. He had everything to offer her. Once he said the words, that would change. She deserved a real man. A man who hadn't been sick.

"I just told you my harrowing story and you didn't go running."

"Nothing you did was wrong. You did everything right. You took care of your daughter. You tried everything to make her well. Anyone would be crushed under the weight of losing a child. No parent should live through that."

"I don't want any credit but thank you for understanding. Whatever is in your past can't possibly bring you more shame than me failing at being a mother."

"You did not fail. If that is what your ex-husband said, he's a fool. Sometimes all our efforts go undone. My mother used to say that God had a plan for us. I didn't really believe her. But maybe she was right." He hadn't thought about his mother's saying in years.

"I'm trying to see the light. You've helped me do that. Let me help you."

"I told you the other day I had cancer. It was testicular cancer." The words vibrated against the walls and off his skin. He hadn't told another living soul before now. No one other than those paid to help take care of him knew of his ordeal.

During treatment, he had sat on the cold tile floor of his bathroom and thrown up until every muscle in his body yelled for him to stop. Faced with surgery, he had paced his house each night, unable to sleep. The doctors had asked if he had a relative or friend who would be there for him. But he had said no each and every time. He didn't want anyone there witnessing what was happening to him. He had the money to pay for care. That was what he had done.

"Oh, Levi. I'm so sorry you had to go through that." She placed her palm on his heated cheek.

He took her hand and laced his fingers with hers. As long as they touched, he could tell her the rest. She was as much a lifeline for him as he was for her.

"It happened. Surprised the hell out of me. But I'm good now. I can go on and live a full life." That was what his doctors had told him. He had been lucky when he looked at the big picture. Luckier than plenty.

He returned to the mattress and motioned for her to follow him. She glanced out the window one more time. Snow mixed with rain fell with speed, coating the grass and the cars.

He wanted to be snowed in tonight and tomorrow and the next day. He wanted to shut out the rest of the world and give him and Skyla a chance to be together without worry or interruptions. The bookstore could wait. Grant could wait. Life could wait.

"Why don't you want anyone to know this? Cancer, unfortunately, is pretty common."

"It's the process that's humiliating. What I was reduced to while trying to get well. I don't want anyone to look at me differently." He eased back against the wall.

"I can understand that. When someone realizes I'm homeless, they look at me with disgust and pity. It's horrible because they don't know any of my story." She snuggled against him, bringing her warmth with her.

He grabbed the blanket and wrapped them in it. He tucked her head under his chin and smelled the clean scent of her hair. He would stay like this all night if she would allow it. They didn't have to do anything. He only wanted to hold her.

"What stupid things someone else thinks is on them, not you."

"Shouldn't I say the same thing to you?"

"Southern male pride."

Her laugh brightened the room. "I don't care that you had cancer. It doesn't change my feelings."

"There's more." He closed his eyes and took a deep breath. Now or never. "I had to have surgery to remove one of my testicles."

She looked up at him. Her eyes narrowed. When he imagined the first time he slept with a woman, he had assumed she would be a fling, something he wasn't serious about. Having no attachment would have made any reaction less brutal. Then he would be ready if the right woman had come along. But he wanted Skyla to remain in his life. When he had returned to Serenity, he hadn't planned on anything past the holidays, but now he wanted it all. The whole picture. The house. The woman. His brother back.

He braced himself for the rejection about to come. She might be understanding, but that would only go so far. He understood. He hadn't wanted to look at himself for weeks.

She slid out of the embrace and turned toward him, her face a neutral mask. She kissed his cheek, then the other, a soft kiss that didn't linger. She would be getting up to leave now so she could find that hotel before the weather became worse.

She stood. Her gaze never left his. He wished she would just get her exit over with so he could pour himself a whiskey and lick his wounds. He had allowed himself to care about this woman too much in too short a time. Expecting her to accept his deformity was a lot to ask anyone. Especially one with her own set of heavy baggage.

He fisted his hands at his sides to keep from grabbing her and begging her to stay. "Skyla—"

"Shh." She placed a finger over his lips. "Not another word."

She pulled her shirt over her head, then shook out that long beautiful hair of hers. She unbuttoned her jeans and slid them to her ankles, stepping out of them. She shivered before him in nothing but a lacy white bra and panties.

She knelt between his legs, then tugged his shirt over his head.

"You don't have to do this." He wanted her hands all over him but hesitated to believe what she was about to do.

"I said no more talking." Her fingers worked his belt free from the buckle.

He stilled her hands with his trembling ones. "Skyla, are you sure?"

"I've never been more sure of anything. I want to see you exactly as you are. Then I want you to make love to me."

Skyla lay with her head against Levi's chest. His heart's rhythm lulled her to sleep, but she didn't want to miss a minute of this night. From the moment she had told him about Emory and the way he accepted her and all her mistakes, she would never want to be with another man.

He had worried about what his cancer had done to his body, but he was no less perfect to her. She didn't care that he had one testicle. She only cared about sharing his bed and his heart.

She adjusted the blanket to cover them better. The fire had dwindled, and the wind continued its pursuit inside the house. They would need some area rugs to keep the draft out. Maybe Levi would agree to heavy curtains they could hang on the windows too. She imagined a completed house filled with joy while she basked in the glow of their evening lovemaking.

"I'll get up and add some wood to the fire," he said.

"No rush. I'm good like this." Her fingers ran across his downy chest hair. She had guessed the hair on his head would be dark brown from his eyebrows and eyelashes and the way his jaw darkened as the day grew long, but now she had confirmation.

"That feels nice." His hand skimmed her back, exciting her all over again.

The snow brightened everything outside, casting a gray glow in the room. She wasn't sure of the hour, but darkness had fallen some time ago.

He tilted her chin and placed a soft kiss on her lips. "Today has been incredible."

It had been. Heat creeped into her cheeks remembering the last couple of hours. No man had ever made love to her the way Levi had. He had taken her to places she didn't know existed more than once.

"I love your hair."

"Thank you. It needs to be cut." She hadn't cut it in at least a year. No money for something like a haircut.

"Never cut it." He turned to look at her. "Hey, what do you think about getting a Christmas tree?"

She hadn't put up a tree in a long time. After Emory,

there had been nothing to celebrate. "I don't know. If you want one. This is your house."

"You're kind of living here too."

"Temporarily. With the bookstore job, I'll be able to pay rent on a regular basis." She may have just fantasized about living here with Levi, but she needed to be practical. Things were too new between them. She could still be a project for him. If he wanted her, he would have to give her space too.

"Are they paying you that much?"

"Enough."

"I'll pay you more." He stiffened. "I shouldn't have said that."

"No." She pushed away from him and reached for her clothes.

"I'm sorry. I didn't mean it that way."

"Sleeping with your boss is never a good idea." She should have known better. What a fool she had become to lie here with this man, a practical stranger, and imagine a future. All he wanted her for was a good time and he had paid her handsomely for it only this morning when he asked her to leave the beach.

That wad of money burned a hole in her coat pocket. She hurried over to the hook by the door and pulled out the cash. "Here."

"I did not sleep with you because I paid you to work around the house. Put that back." He sat up and the blanket fell to his waist.

She wanted to believe him, especially after sharing their stories. But life had taught her that no amount of wanting something made it happen. "I can't take your money if we're going to sleep together. Either you take it back or we stop right here."

"Don't make it sound like that." He pulled on his jeans.

"Like what?"

"Like what we did was sordid. Because it wasn't." He tugged a shirt over his head.

"It was too lonely people finding comfort in each other." That had to be all it was for him. He was lonely. He had said as much. She was lonely too.

"It was more than that to me." Hurt flashed across his eyes.

"How could it be?"

"I think I'm in love with you." He took a step toward her.

"Don't say that." She held up her hand to stop him from coming any closer.

"Why not? If it's true."

"Because we don't know each other well enough to be saying things about love."

"I'm not in high school. I think I know how I feel. I just beat cancer and have a second chance at living. I learned the hard way that I had better take life by the balls. No pun intended. Or maybe I did intend it. I'm not getting another go at this. When I know what I want, I'm going for it. No more hesitation. For the first time in my life, I'm allowing myself to feel my emotions."

"I don't care how you feel. I won't take money from you and have sex with you."

"Why not? Every married couple makes trade-offs like that."

"You don't understand me at all. And you definitely don't love me." She would sleep in the extra bedroom under her blankets on the cold floor. He could sleep out here by the fire. In the morning, when the weather passed, she would find that hotel room.

"I do love you. Don't tell me how I feel. It's okay if you don't love me back. But you will."

"You're mighty confident of yourself."

"I am after what just happened between us. No one can be that vulnerable with someone they don't trust." He arched a brow.

Her cheeks heated up again. "Unfair play."

"Don't run from me. We'll figure out the work thing. Okay?"

Before she could agree or disagree with him, an orange glow moved outside the window as if caught in the wind.

"What is that?" Levi went to the window. "Call 911. Melvin's house is on fire."

Chapter Sixteen

The Serenity by the Sea firefighters put out the last of the flames. They had arrived in minutes before the fire could take hold of much. The snow and freezing rain had aided in keeping the fire at bay. Snow continued to fall, but the wind had given up some of its hold.

Levi stood beside Melvin who shook with fury and not the cold if the muttering under his breath was any indication. He had been out visiting his daughter when the fire started.

Levi had called Melvin right after the 911 call and he raced back to see his home devoured by flames.

"Who set fire to my house?" Melvin said loud enough anyone a mile away would have heard.

Captain Wright dressed in his fire gear, with soot on his face, approached them. "Melvin, we don't know that yet, but the source was the Christmas tree." Captain Wright turned to him with an outstretched hand. "Nice to see you again. Do you live on this street?"

"I live in the last house." He shook.

"Did you see anyone, Levi?"

"Only saw the glow of the flames. That's when we called for help."

"Who's we?" Captain Wright looked around.

"My friend. She's inside."

"I'll want to talk with her. Melvin, we'll have a full report in a few days. Can you stay with your daughter until then?"

"Yeah. Yeah. I can stay with my daughter and her family. Can I get inside to grab a few things? The bedrooms don't look like they were hit."

"Someone will escort you when you're ready. Just shout." Captain Wright gave Levi a curt nod and walked away.

Melvin glared at Levi. "Was Skyla with you all day?"

"Come on, Melvin. You don't really think it was her, do you?"

"She's living two doors down from me. Was about to take a plunge into that frigid river. Maybe she doesn't have a lot to live for and she's going to take a few people with her."

"You're off base here."

"Were you with her all day?"

"Not all day, no. But we have been together since late afternoon right up until now. Whoever set your tree on fire would have done it within minutes of the whole thing going up. It wasn't her."

"And she never left your side the whole time? She couldn't have slipped out while you were asleep maybe?"

"Not a chance." They had been too busy getting to know each other to sleep. He smiled at the memory.

Melvin arched a brow. "Pretty big grin. She your girl-friend or something?"

"Something. It's too early to put a name to it. But I promise you, Skyla isn't the arsonist."

"If you say you were together, I guess I have to believe you. Don't like the timing of it all."

He didn't either. Anyone else could think the fires were started by Skyla too. He would defend her to anyone who questioned her.

Melvin kicked the dirt. "Tell Skyla thanks for calling it in. You hear?"

"No thanks needed, Melvin. Just glad you're okay."

"I better get my belongings." Melvin ambled toward Captain Wright who handed Melvin off to someone else to help him inside the house.

Levi wasn't ready to go back to the cottage just yet. He wished he knew who would want to harm people at Christmas or at any time. The houses back here made easy targets. The arsonist most likely slipped inside Melvin's, lit the tree, and was gone in minutes.

Whoever had done this could have looked in his front window and seen him and Skyla making love. He didn't have window coverings, but he never imagined anyone would come down here. He had to believe nothing bad would happen to either of them, but bad things happened all the time.

He checked his phone. The early morning hours were upon them. He'd been given another day. He wouldn't waste it. He wanted to take this time to appreciate all he did have in his life. Everything could be taken away in an instant. He knew that firsthand from losing Emmett to his own cancer diagnosis. One minute he had felt fine except for the lump he had found and the next he was a cancer patient. His whole life had turned on its head in a flash.

The fire trucks pulled away, leaving muddy tracks on the road. The snow turned red in their rear lights. Melvin came out with a travel bag and slid into his car, probably to return to his daughter's house for the night.

The cops would want to know who might have a grudge against Melvin. He was a nice, older man. As for neighbors, Levi had a lot worse in his day. But he didn't know Melvin at all other than the few words they had spoken. Melvin could have wronged anyone in his long life.

Or was this person lighting Christmas trees on fire choosing random victims? If Levi purchased a tree and placed it in the front window, would his house be next?

He might not have cared a few weeks ago, but now he wanted this house. And he wanted Skyla inside it, sleeping beside him night after night.

Levi turned for the house but stopped. One truck remained parked at the far end of the road, closer to Melvin's house. In the dark, it took him a minute to recognize the vehicle.

Grant slid out from the driver's side and marched over to him. He wore a red parka and jeans. Duck boots on his feet. The kind they used to wear fishing.

"What are you doing here?" he said before Grant could make it all the way. He wasn't in the mood for another fight.

His body ached and his eyes itched from the smoke and lack of sleep. He wanted to go inside now and curl up against Skyla, pull her to him, make love to her again because right now he needed to feel alive, and she made him that way. Grant would only remind him of his mistakes. Those memories could wait for tomorrow.

"I heard there was a fire over here. I came to check it out."

"Is Melvin a friend of yours?"

"Don't know Melvin. Was that his house that caught fire?"

"It was. You probably won't want to admit it, but you came for me." He hadn't expected that and didn't want to read too much into it either.

"I just wanted to make sure you didn't die."

"Why? Because you want another chance to tell me how much you don't want me here?"

"I don't want you here, but you are, and you won't leave no matter what I say. Kassidy told me I have to learn to exist in this town with you. I'm hoping you get bored and leave like you always do."

"I'm sticking this time, brother. I like it here." The town suited him with its bodies of water and residents who cared about one another. He hadn't lived in a place like this before.

"Figures."

"Well, you can see I'm still standing. So I'm going inside where it's warm. You should go back to your family."

"Your house sucks."

He had to agree. "For now. But I'm working on it."

"Who'd you hire? Someone from town?"

"No one yet. Why do you care?"

"Just asking." Grant glanced at his boots, then back up.

"Why are you really here at this late hour in the snow?"

"Got wind of the fire. Wanted to make sure you didn't burn to a crisp right before Christmas. But that doesn't change things between us. You're still a liar."

"I love you too."

"No one said anything about that. I'm still mad at you and always will be. You can't change that even if your house did go up in flames." Grant wrinkled his nose and turned on his heel.

Levi waited until he was near the truck. "You're coming around. I knew you would."

Grant gave him the finger.

Everyone was talking about the fire at Melvin's two days ago. Skyla sat in the corner at Bella Notte bakery with a tattered paperback that couldn't keep her attention. The whispers floating around her like the smell of baked bread had her leaving the story of a sinking ship and its passengers for the gossip of Serenity by the Sea.

Speculation ran over various people like a giant truck. Names of those accused were unfamiliar to her except for Todd from the hardware store. Levi had mentioned he'd met Todd recently. She'd have to ask Levi if he thought Todd would be a fit for the arsonist.

Anyone could be doing this awful thing. Even someone

from another town could come in and wreak havoc on their small paradise. She couldn't be sure if she had heard correctly, but someone in line may have said her name in connection to the fires.

She was quickly becoming the talk of the town. That wasn't how she wanted to be known. Not as the homeless woman who had lost her only child. Not as Levi's charity case, though it was hard to argue that she wasn't at the moment. She would not mind being known as a Russo sister even if she had a different last name.

Residents would find it more palatable to accuse an outsider than one of their own. And she was definitely an outsider.

Working at the bookstore would help, but it would take time to win over the year-rounders who had ties to the town for generations. She may not even be in town long enough for that to happen. Her future was unknown. Today was the only day she could count on. And even that teetered on an unsteady ledge.

The line at the pastry case never shortened. People wanted their sweets either for this moment to savor or were ordering for the holidays. A small woman behind the counter that patrons called Sophia or Momma D barked orders to the men in the back and smiled wide for her customers, offering them what seemed like terms of endearment in Italian.

Sophia reminded Skyla of a sweet grandmother. She never had one of those and wondered if Bailey and her sisters knew their paternal grandmother.

Colin, the customer from the bookstore who never

bought a book, came through the door. Skyla made eye contact with him and offered a small wave.

He nodded in return and joined the line.

She decided to take a chance and slipped from the chair, leaving her book behind to let everyone else know the table was still taken.

"Hi, Colin. I'm Skyla from the bookstore."

"I know who you are." He gave her the once-over.

Her clothes weren't new, but they were clean. She didn't judge his stained barn jacket or shirt underneath with the frayed collar or the paperback in his hand as tattered and worn as hers.

"It's nice to see you. If you're staying to have a pastry, you can join me."

He narrowed his eyes. "No, thank you. I'm here to read."

"You can read. I won't bother you. It's just that it's pretty busy today and the tables are hard to come by."

"No, thank you."

"Did you hear about the fire at Melvin's?" She would try the approach everyone else was using this morning.

"I heard." He kept his gaze on the front of the line.

She wanted to tap him on the shoulder to get him to look in her direction, but she refrained. Colin didn't seem like the kind of person who wanted to be touched.

"It's a shame, isn't it?"

"What is?" He glanced back at her. Finally.

"Melvin's house at this time of year."

"I don't like Christmas. It's too noisy." He moved up in line, giving her his back.

She would chalk that up to his strange social skills and returned to her table.

She had snuck out of the cottage this morning while Levi was still asleep. She had left a note by the coffee maker, explaining she needed to run some errands, but he hadn't texted any kind of reply or that he had even seen the note.

What errands those would be, she had no clue. Someone like her didn't run errands, but she did need to get out of the house. Sleeping next to Levi, curling up against his warm body, was the best Christmas present ever. For the first time in years, the cold hadn't invaded her bones while she slept.

But she was getting too used to the comforts of that house, as uncomfortable as it was sleeping on an air mattress in those drafty rooms. Levi had offered her shelter and food. Two things that she had struggled with for months. If he ended things with her before she was ready to leave, she'd be in worse shape than before he found her in the woods. Before he rescued her, she could do her miserable life for a while longer. She had become used to it. But now, she didn't know how to go back to living only in her car, eating cold food out of cans, working odd jobs to make some money.

A conversation from the line of customers waiting to be served drifted toward her. She put down her book again.

"If you ask me, it's that guy that bought that abandoned house out on River Road. Who else would have known Melvin wasn't home?" A woman wearing a burgundy knit cap and matching long puffer coat that cut off at her calves said to the woman in line next to her.

"I heard that was Grant Hawkins' brother. He wouldn't do something like that, would he?"

"Grant wouldn't be the first person to have a sibling who was a criminal." The women moved up in line.

They suspected Levi? That was almost as absurd as suspecting her. But these women didn't know them. Skyla glanced around the bakery. A few people dropped their gazes when she looked their way. Serenity by the Sea residents wanted someone to blame and pointing the finger at two strangers frightened them less than the arsonist hiding among one of their own.

The bakery became too warm. She shoved her book in her bag, next to the DNA results, and hurried outside into the cold air. Wind whipped against her as she struggled into her coat. Snow still covered grassy surfaces.

For once she wanted a fair shake, the chance to prove herself before being judged by others who did not understand the first damn thing about her life.

The police needed to find the person responsible for setting Christmas trees on fire before she became the guilty party simply because she didn't fit in around here.

"Skyla." The voice came from behind her, as startling as the breeze.

She swung around. Bailey waved from the boardwalk. Her white knit cap with matching pom-pom sparkled in the sun.

Her cropped coat lifted when she waved, revealing her skin and what might be a belly ring, but Skyla couldn't tell from across the street. Bailey's wide legged pants ended in chunky brown boots.

Bailey hurried across the road. "Are you going into the bakery? I'm dying for one of Mr. D's éclairs. Want to join?"

"Thanks. I just came from there. Were you on the beach?" She shouldn't be surprised to find anyone who lived in this town making time to walk the sand.

"I was. Like usual." Bailey rolled her eyes as if to tease herself. "I had to search for sea glass this morning. I'm sure you've noticed it's been a crazy week at the store. I look to relax. It's like a meditation for me."

"You have a lot going on with the holidays and the expansion."

"True, but Jack and I keep bumping heads. I hate arguing with him."

"Do you want to talk about it?"

"I don't want to bother you with this. I didn't mean to even bring it up."

"Come on. Let's get those éclairs. My treat." She gripped Bailey's arm before she could decline Skyla's offer. An offer she should not have made because she shouldn't be spending money on desserts, but this was her chance to bond with Bailey.

The line moved quickly and the two of them found a table vacated by a mother and her toddler.

"So, tell me what's going on."

"Okay. It's our first holiday together and we have very different ideas about how to celebrate, decorate, shop. You name it." Bailey took a bite of her éclair.

"Which way are you leaning?"

"I just wanted some peace and quiet. We've been so busy since the summer, and with all that is happening in town, I wanted to skip the tree and the decorations. But Jack says we can't let the arsonist win."

"I can understand your point, but Jack might have a point too." Skyla forced herself to eat with purpose and not shove the custard-filled pastry into her mouth all in one piece. She had never eaten an éclair before and would not embarrass herself by saying so. The chocolate on top made her mouth salivate. The sugar went straight to her head.

"About the arsonist?"

"You could get a small tabletop tree this year. The rumor mill says the arsonist is only after real trees."

"You think I'm overreacting." Bailey wiped her hand on a napkin.

"No, not at all. I'm scared about the fires too, but I've learned I'm scared most of the time anyway. If I'm going to live, I have to get used to that." She decided to take her treat home and share it with Levi later.

"Good advice. What are you afraid of?"

"Everything." She laughed to hide the truth and Bailey laughed along.

"You're not eating your éclair."

"One bite was enough for now." She wrapped it in a napkin and hoped that didn't seem weird.

"That's how you stay so thin. I don't have that kind of willpower."

Bailey would if she was forced to, but Skyla kept that to herself.

"Will you work things out with Jack?"

"I hope so. We're just so different. He's very particular,

and I like to wing it. Sometimes that doesn't work out well. I'm sorry. I really shouldn't be dumping all my stuff on you."

"No problem. I like talking with you." She hoped saying that wasn't too weird either.

Bailey offered a warm smile. "You know, I like you too."

"You didn't mention. Did you find any sea glass by the water?" She had come to the beach once as a child, but her mother didn't even want to go in the ocean. Skyla had seen tons of pictures of sea glass, but never a real piece up close.

"Not a single tiny piece. It's so much harder these days. When my dad was younger, he would collect sea glass from all over. He had tons of it."

Skyla savored this piece of information, then tucked it away. Her father loved sea glass. "What did he do with it?"

"He left it to us. Unfortunately. Well, Maren and Kassidy think it's great. They tried to sell some of it to collectors. The rare colors, anyway. They display some of it in their homes. My niece, Peyton, she makes art out of it and sells it. But there was so much, it's in Kassidy's attic."

"I would love to see the pieces sometime." The words were out before she could stop them.

"Are you a collector?" Bailey narrowed her eyes.

"Me? No. Just an admirer."

"So, tell me." Bailey leaned forward. "Are you and Levi just boss and employee or is there something more?"

"You don't like him." Even if they hadn't defined what was happening between them, he was more than any boss she'd ever had.

"I didn't mean for it to sound like a judgment. I'm just curious. Nosey is more like it."

"We didn't plan for our relationship to grow. I don't want to continue to work for him now that our situation has changed, but he insists I finish what I've started." That was true. She hadn't planned anything except to get from one hour to the next before her arrival in Serenity.

"Are you working on a special project?" Bailey picked at her dessert.

"His house. I'm fixing it up." She loved the idea of taking something old and tired and bringing it back to life. She had color ideas for the walls and thoughts about the kind of furniture that would work in a small cottage on the lake. She'd preserve as much of the real wood as possible because of its charm.

"I work for Jack."

"How does that make you feel?"

Bailey wiped her hands on a napkin again, then placed them in her lap. "In all honesty, I don't like it. We have trouble separating work from home. When we're home, I want us to talk about stuff besides the bookstore. All he wants to talk about is the store and the expansion, the financials, you name it."

"And you want to talk about the books you're reading, your future with him, right?" Skyla remembered those days with Will when they were young and full of hope. They had planned for a future that never arrived. Instead, their last lengthy conversations were about doctors, hospitals, medications, cancer, and dying. She had never realized before now that long before they had lost Emory, they had lost each other.

"Exactly. He says because we're running a business,

there are moments outside of work hours where we have to talk about work. He says not everything can be fun and games. I suppose he's right sometimes."

"Is there a way to compromise?"

Bailey stuck her finger in the éclair crème and licked it off. "You're good at seeing both sides. If we want to make this thing between us work, we'll have to figure out a way for both of us to get what we want. Should it really be this hard right off the bat?"

"I'm not the right one to ask. My marriage ended in disaster." She hadn't meant to let that slip. The sugar must have short-circuited her brain. The less Bailey knew about Skyla's past, the better. At least for now. Having to tell the parts that involved Emory would be too much and too soon.

"What happened? If you don't mind me asking."

"That is a story for another day. I'm sorry. I have to run. I forgot about an appointment. It was great to spend time with you." She pushed out of the chair and grabbed her backpack.

"You too. I'll see you at the bookstore tomorrow."

"Tomorrow." Skyla hurried out of the store and down the street to where she parked the car. She glanced over her shoulder to make sure Bailey didn't follow.

The only thing at her back was the wind, shoving her closer to the truth because lies wouldn't hold up forever.

And when those truths were told... she'd be left tumbling in the windstorm.

Chapter Seventeen

Skyla stared at him with wide eyes, a smirk on those full lips. "Please, Levi. Let's get a Christmas tree and a few strands of lights. We don't even have to do ornaments."

The excitement on her face from the prospect of a tree lit up the room. She needed this one small win, but a tree was the one thing he couldn't give her. If the arsonist was trying to scare everyone in this town, he or she had sunk their claws deep into Levi.

"What got into you?" Levi took her in. Her cheeks flushed pink beneath her cream-colored skin. Her red hair hung over her shoulders in soft waves and almost to her elbows. He tried not to think about his hands in it because he would much rather take her to bed than have this discussion. But those green eyes flecked with brown turned his world on its head.

"It's Christmas and I have a lot to be grateful for. Namely you. I just want to celebrate that." She flopped onto the mattress still in the living room in front of the dormant fireplace and sat cross-legged.

"Did Bailey put this idea in your head? She's the one always floating around like life's one big fluffy cloud. Like she's some kind of sprite or something, spreading glitter, all twinkling."

"You don't like Bailey?"

"No. No. I like her just fine. I mean... I don't really know her that well, but when I was here last time, I had no reason to dislike her."

"Why don't you want a tree?"

This woman would not be deterred, and he had to admire that quality even if in this moment it caused a pain in his backside.

"I just don't want a tree." Because someone might come here and set it on fire. He didn't want to take that chance that his new house, new to him anyway, would go up in flames. This house with all its flaws was the first risk he had taken since his illness. Buying anything in this town with Grant not speaking to him could have been a risk that would have failed on a major scale, but he went ahead and bought the worst house in Serenity anyway. Even though the house sucked, he wanted to live here.

Serenity by the Sea offered a quiet place to settle into. Where the year-round residents watched out for each other because they knew their neighbors, knew the families they belonged to. He never had that in his life and had been envious of Grant, finding it the way he had. Levi wanted a chance at some of that peace. He was close now and he didn't want some arsonist taking it away from him.

"Are you worried about what happened to Melvin?"

He glanced out the front window. Gray clouds had rolled in on the wind again. The damp coastal air continued to sneak in through all the drafty places in the house. He went to the thermostat on the wall and turned up the heat.

"I don't think anyone would be dumb enough to come back to this street a second time and hit the only other house." He was worried that exact thing would happen, but he didn't want to tell Skyla that and make her afraid too.

"Are you against Christmas trees?"

"I'm not against them. I just don't want one this year. The house isn't ready for it."

"The house could use some cheering up."

"Skyla, can you drop the tree thing?"

She glanced away from him. "Is it because you don't want to spend the money on one? I understand. It's not like I can contribute to a tree or anything. I shouldn't have..."

Her words floated away on a whisper. He went to her and took her cold hands in his, but she kept her gaze away from him.

"Look at me, Skyla. Please."

She turned her watery gaze his way. He ran his thumb over her cheek, stopping the single tear.

"This isn't about the money or who's paying. I know this is modern times and all, but I was raised to be a provider for the woman in my life. That's a man's job. Even if you made more money than I did, I'd still want to pay for everything and tell you to keep your money."

"That's very old-fashioned." Her laugh was interrupted by a sniffle.

"I know. But I don't care, darling. Stop worrying about money. When you get on your feet again, you can buy me a cup of coffee, okay?"

"How do you know I'll get on my feet again?"

"I just do."

"Levi, what is happening between us? It's so new and a little scary and yet it feels right. How can that be?"

"That I don't have an answer for. I don't need one either. Neither of us is promising a future to the other. We're just enjoying what we have right now. If and when that changes, then we'll figure out what's happening."

"I've never been good at taking risks."

"Leave that to me. Before my cancer, I was too good at taking risks. That's how I ended up in a tussle with Grant."

"Are you ready to talk about that yet?"

"Nothing to talk about. I made a mistake in our work. He's not ready to forgive me."

"There's more to it than that."

If he told her, what would she think of him, a man who lied to his own brother? "I'll promise you this much. I'll never do it again."

She rewarded him with a smile, but her shoulders sagged. "All right. Keep your secret. And you can forget about the tree. I understand. You just don't want one."

"How about a compromise?"

"What kind?"

"We get a tree. You can decorate it however you want, but we keep it outside." They could set it up away from the house. By the river, maybe. He saw outlets by the shed. If the power worked, they could run an extension cord and Skyla could have her lights.

With the tree away from this house and the few things he held dear at the moment, the arsonist wouldn't have any power over him.

Levi worried the arsonist already did.

"What do you say? Are you willing to keep the tree outside?"

She gnawed on her bottom lip. "You are worried the arsonist will come back and set our tree on fire."

He hesitated and that was his mistake.

"It's okay to be scared. I've been scared a good part of my adult life." She hopped off the mattress and came to him, wrapping her arms around his neck.

"Before the cancer, I was never scared. Nothing to be scared about. I had faced many demons and always walked away. I thought when cancer got me, my good luck had changed. But I won again. At some point I'm going to lose. And I'm not willing to lose this house. Or you."

She kissed him then and he pushed aside thoughts of worry and loss.

For now.

The Christmas tree lot was absent of people and full of trees. Even though the sun had found rest in the west, it was only five o'clock in the evening. The lot on the front lawn of the town theater should have been bustling with buyers this close to Christmas.

Instead, it seemed forgotten. She was sorry for the trees that wouldn't find a home this year, but she was hopeful for herself. Getting a tree was a big move for her. She hadn't had one since Emory and didn't think she ever would again. This taste of living again chipped away at some of the ice around her broken heart.

"Where is everyone?" she said.

"If I had to take a guess, no one in town wants a tree this year." Levi held her hand as they walked down the first aisle of blue spruces.

"That's sad. The guy at the register looks upset or bored maybe."

"That's Kevin Wright, the fire department captain. Melvin told me his grandfather started this Christmas tree lot decades ago."

"You and Melvin were gossiping?" She had no idea why that was adorable.

"Who else am I going to talk to? You're my only other friend in town." He flashed her his devilish smile.

"There's Todd from the hardware store." She gripped Levi's arm and tugged him. "Do you think Todd is the arsonist?"

He burst out laughing, but when she didn't laugh back, his face dropped. "You think it's Todd? Why?" Levi leaned in and whispered in her ear.

"I overheard people talking in the bakery."

"But that's just rumor."

"It might be, or it might not."

"Let's go down another row. I don't want to bump into

Kevin." Levi pulled her three rows down where the Douglas Fir stood.

Christmas music played from speakers attached to poles where vines of lights draped as they walked between the rows of trees and their magical cedar scent.

Levi gave her hand a squeeze. That fire at Melvin's could have been in their house while they were making love. She was finally planting some roots that might take hold for the first time in years. She couldn't lose that to some reckless person who did not care about anyone else. Losing Levi, after so much other loss in her life, would destroy her in ways she could not imagine. Did not want to imagine.

She could close her eyes and pretend that the past didn't exist for a second. That choosing the perfect tree was a tradition of theirs. Something they would have started years ago when they were young and full of hope, before Levi's cancer, before her tragedy. A tradition they would carry with them until they were too old to amble through the trees without the assistance of a kind hand or a sturdy cane.

She missed her child every second, could not imagine a world where Emory wasn't a part of, but Skyla needed some moments, small as they were, to be free of the pain and suffering. She could taste the familiar feeling of joy when she was with Levi.

Each day her guard crumbled a little more. Soon it would not be able to protect her from heartbreak. She would be safer wading into the ocean, fully dressed, during a storm than falling for a man she hardly knew.

A fat Douglas Fir caught her eye. "What do you think of

this one?" The needles were soft between her fingers. The tree stood about five feet tall. She didn't need a huge tree. Only one that she could see from the window.

She had agreed to keeping the tree outside even if the idea hurt a little. Levi had been honest with her about his fears. She needed to respect that. When she finally told him about her DNA results, she wanted him to respect her fears too.

"It's not very tall." Levi stood next to it. The tree came up to his shoulder.

"Not everyone is blessed with your height."

"Do you like my height?" He gripped her waist and pulled her against his hard chest.

"I have no complaints." He was the most handsome man she had ever been with, but if he had been shorter than her, she would not have cared. His heart was big and generous and kind. His being a good person was the most important trait.

"If you like this tiny tree, then we'll get this one." He placed a kiss on the tip of her nose.

"Let's look around a bit more. I love walking along the aisles and smelling the trees." She hurried up the row, anxious to see every tree, give each one a chance to win her heart.

When she was a little girl, her mother had found a tabletop tree with silver branches in the dumpster behind their apartment building. Her mother had taken the tree, brushed off the garbage, and put it in the window of their living room. Not all the lights on it worked, but that was their tree for the next three years.

Skyla's fingers skipped across the fresh branches as she went along the aisle. She had meant what she said earlier to Levi about being grateful. This was the best night she'd had in a long time.

"Hey, wait up," Levi shouted behind her.

She turned the corner at the end of the row. The song changed to "Blue Christmas." Not one of her favorites, but she would not let the song discourage her. The wind decided then to bustle in and stir the trees, dropping cold air onto her. She glanced over her shoulder to see if Levi was coming and collided into a mass.

She bounced and fell on her butt. Pain shot up from her tailbone. Her hat slipped over her eyes and her backpack tumbled from her arm.

"I'm sorry. I didn't see you." A familiar male voice descended upon her. "Are you okay?"

A hand was around her elbow, pulling her to her feet. She brushed the hat away from her face. Where was her bag?

"What happened?" Levi came up beside her out of breath.

"I bumped into her," Grant said.

Her heart sank. Grant would ruin their evening and there was nothing she could do about his presence at the lot and what it would do to Levi. She should have agreed to the small tree. They would have been going in the opposite direction toward the register and Kevin Wright to pay. She would never have bumped into Levi's brother on this splendid evening.

"It was nothing. I wasn't paying attention. I'm sorry I

bumped into you." She retrieved her bag from the ground. Nothing had fallen out.

"It was an accident," Grant said. "Glad you're okay. But if you'll excuse me, my wife and daughter are looking for me. Have a nice evening."

Levi watched as his brother walked away. Pain darkened his eyes.

"Why don't you try and talk to him?"

"He doesn't want to talk to me. That's obvious. Come on. Let's go."

Her fingers dug into the down of his coat sleeve. She gripped his bicep. "Tell me, Levi. Tell me what happened. Maybe I can help you fix it. I can see what this fight with your brother is doing to you."

He regarded her. She could almost see the wheels turning behind his eyes, but she stayed quiet. He would have to decide for himself if he could share his pain with her. And if he couldn't, what would that say about this strange thing between them?

"Let's buy the tree and put it up. Then I'll tell you. I promise."

Chapter Eighteen

He had to admit... the small tree held a big punch. Levi had stretched two extension cords from the shed, where the power miraculously worked, to the tree they put up closer to the river and far enough away from the house that if it should catch fire, the flames would never make it across the yard.

That shed would be a project he and Skyla would take on together. He no longer had any interest in her working for him. He wanted to be her partner. She had to be ready for that and though her feelings seemed pretty obvious, she wasn't done working through her grief. He wasn't so blind and dumb he couldn't tell. She needed more time, and time was all he had these days.

At some point, he'd have to think about a new career. Music was over for him. He conquered his goals, kicked some ass, and then the industry kicked his ass back.

When Skyla had agreed to keep the tree outside for him, he knew he had made the right decision to rescue her from the woods. She trusted him. For that he was grateful because she was the only one.

He had built a small fire down by the river in an old metal fire pit he'd found in the shed. The fire gave off heat while they decorated the tree with pinecones and the lights plugged into the power cords. He wanted to show her in as many ways as possible that he was a man of his word. Because before now, he wasn't.

"Do you like the tree?" He already knew the answer but wanted to ask just to see her face light up brighter than the fat moon over the water.

"It's beautiful. Thank you for getting it."

"Thank you for always finding the best in every situation."

"It's hard sometimes, but I try." She ran her fingers over the tree branch.

"You seem to have found the best in me. I don't know how you did it. Every other woman in my life has only seen the worst in me, honestly."

"Then they were blind. From the minute you asked me inside your house, you showed me the very best of you."

"Do you want to sit by the fire for a minute or go inside?" He had also dragged two chairs from the shed that looked as if they would hold their weight by the fire.

"Let's stay out a little longer. I know it's freezing, but I want to be near the tree."

"Will you sit with me?"

She took the seat beside him. He wanted to hold her hand for his comfort, but after he told her the story of why

Grant was mad at him, she might not want to touch him again.

"I want to tell you about my fight with Grant."

"I'm listening."

"What I'm about to tell you isn't me anymore." He didn't even like to think about how he used to behave. "Getting sick helped me become someone else, someone better."

"There is nothing you can say that will change my mind about you."

"I hope that's true." He poked at the fire with a long stick. The embers came to life, encouraging him to keep going.

"Several years ago, Grant owed some songs to the record label who had signed him. It's a long story so I won't bore you with the whys and the hows. But he had refused to give them all of the songs contracted. He told me, as his manager, to figure out a way to get the label off his back."

"I'm taking a guess that you didn't do as he asked."

The day Grant told him he wouldn't submit those songs, Levi had wanted to put his fist through the wall. Grant was his biggest client, and Levi had stood to lose a lot of money if that contract was voided. He had been tired by then of Grant hiding from the world and pushing him away. Levi had lost a brother too. He had been in pain just like Grant, but Levi had not run from the world in an attempt to hide from the emptiness caused by Emmett's death.

"I didn't know how to get the label to back off. I tried everything I could think of, but the execs were prepared to sue us and neither of us had the kind of capital we would need when we lost. And we would have lost. Dead in the water if they went after us."

"I understand not wanting to lose everything. When it feels like the ground under you is collapsing with every move, you'll scramble to grab on to anything solid to prevent the inevitable." She glanced toward the tree. The lights reflected in her eyes, giving her a glow as if from the inside.

"What am I doing?" He was complaining about his life to a woman who had nothing. "You don't have to hear this. Your problems are bigger than mine."

She slid her hand into his. "We aren't comparing who has the biggest scars. You've suffered, and I want to know your story. I won't judge you for making mistakes. Please keep telling me."

He hesitated. The story was ugly and showed the worst side of him. Not exactly the way to impress a woman, but the intensity in her gaze encouraged him to go forward.

"Grant didn't care if we were sued, but I did. I had nothing but my managing business. Grant was starting a whole new life. He had left me on the side of the road like garbage, and I was mad. I'd lost enough after Emmett died, and Grant stopped playing. I wasn't going to lose my shirt too.

"So, I wrote the songs myself and told the record label executives they were from Grant. The songs ran up the charts. The downloads were nonstop. I couldn't believe it. I thought they'd get a little play and flop like everything else I'd ever written. I was just trying to stop from ending up hom—" He bit down on the rest of the word and wanted to kick himself for even thinking it.

"Homeless. It's okay. You can say it. I don't want to be homeless. That wasn't my plan or my goal. I hate living in my car. I just made one too many mistakes."

"I'm sorry for having such a big mouth." He didn't want to hurt her. And that scared him. She had become important to him in no time at all. If someone had told him they had fallen for a woman they had just met, he would have insisted they were nuts. He had never experienced deep emotions for any woman until now. He had cared about other women, made sure they were treated with respect, but the unexplainable thing between him and Skyla was nothing he could have imagined.

"Don't be sorry for speaking your mind. Go on. Tell me the rest."

"If you're sure."

She placed a soft kiss on his cheek, and he wanted to fold her into his arms, forget about this whole conversation, and make love to her out here by the fire near this tree she loved.

"Okay then. Every music outlet wanted an interview with Grant. Radio stations, online sites, podcasts, everyone. The label started breathing down my back to get Grant to write more songs and do a tour."

"Why is this bad?"

"Well, for one, saying Grant wrote those songs when Grant had not written those songs was a violation of our contract. I impersonated him. The label could have gone after me for fraud, which was a risk I shouldn't have taken, but I thought the chances of them catching on were slim. I also thought when Grant saw the success of the songs, he would be okay with what I did. He got all the credit."

"But he wasn't okay."

"Grant did not appreciate that I had said I was him to give a label his work when that label never had our backs. He didn't want to be in the public eye anymore. Not like he was. That was another thing he wanted me to make the label understand, but by handing in those songs, I had done the opposite."

"Are you telling me that Grant never heard the songs on the radio or streaming apps?"

"Grant had no idea. He wasn't paying attention because he was here with Kassidy and happier than he had ever been. But I had to tell him because everyone was looking for him again.

"When I did tell him, he was so mad that he decked me."

"He hit you?" Her eyebrows shot into her hairline.

"I kind of had it coming." He hadn't even put his hands up to defend himself. He had lied to his brother and put them in a worse situation than if he had just stood his ground against the label in the first place.

"If you don't mind me saying, I think your brother over-reacted and should have been more appreciative of your help. Violence is never the answer."

He stood and scooped her into his arms. Her warmth seeped into him. He hadn't noticed how cold he was, sitting outside and making his story tangible. She wrapped her arms around his waist and snuggled closer.

"How many times have you apologized?"

"A ton. I tried to give him the royalty money, hoping that would make up for what I did, but he sent it back. I told him he was being an asshole. He told me to screw off."

"Did the label find out?" She eased out of the embrace and took his hand.

"No. Grant agreed not to tell them, but he also said he would never talk to me again. He said I never had his back and that proved it."

"Do you mind if we go inside to finish this conversation?"

He led her toward the house. They stepped into the kitchen and tossed their coats on the counter.

"What about more songs and the tour? How did you get out of that?"

"We were never contracted for more than those three songs. I told them Grant was out and there wasn't much they could do." Grant wasn't the first musician to write bad songs to get out of a contract, but Levi had been greedy. He wanted those songs to make money. He hadn't planned on Grant's reaction. Another mistake.

"What did you do after Grant said he would never talk to you again?"

"I ignored him. At least that's what I told myself. He was the one ignoring me. I went about my business. I repped clients. I made money. I toured around the world for two years. Until I got the diagnosis. Then my world stopped short, and I wanted to fix things with my brother."

"But he won't let you."

"Nope. So I bought this dump of a house in the town where he lived to force him to deal with me. Do you want some tea?" He reached for the kettle, but she nudged him away.

"Sure. So, here you are in Serenity and Grant's still not talking to you."

"I regret what I did now. But I didn't then. I didn't see any way out of our predicament except to lie to the record label."

"What if the label had caught you? Wouldn't you have been in more trouble than if Grant had just refused to hand in the songs?" She turned on the stove's flame.

"Probably, but I knew I could write three good songs. Not chart toppers, but better than the crap he had slapped down on the page. No one was going to listen to those, and the label would have rejected them. I didn't know the songs would hit, but once that happened, I didn't think the label would care who wrote them. They had made money. I just hadn't planned on Grant being so mad."

"Why didn't you tell him ahead of time?"

"Because I was arrogant."

"But that's changed. You are the kindest, most selfless person I have ever met." She held his gaze with her watery one.

He went to her, closing the space between them because he had to be near her. She understood him in ways no one else ever did.

"I don't know about selfless. But having a terminal illness, even if the odds of beating it are in your favor, knocks any arrogance out of you like a blow from an unde-feated prize fighter. When I believed I would die, every bad choice I had ever made had swelled up in my head until I thought it would explode. Everything I thought was important before became as insignificant as the rocks in that massive river out there."

"Life threw you a curveball, but you didn't strike out," she said with a nod.

"You like baseball?"

"A little."

"I do too. So, nothing I've said has changed your mind about me?"

"If anything, it's only made me care about you more."

He kissed her because he couldn't wait any longer to taste the sweetness on her tongue. She accepted him. And he, her. This was the place he had been searching for, a place where a woman would see him for who he was, faults and all, and not run. And in turn he had found a woman who was honest and decent and didn't want anything from him except his affection.

"Let me show you what you mean to me." And he kissed her again.

Chapter Nineteen

Skyla wiped the sweat from her eyes. She had unpacked boxes of books and rearranged shelves all day. Her back ached and her thighs quivered from all the squats and ladder climbing. She was starving and tired. All she could think about was going back to Levi's and crashing on his new furniture due to arrive today.

She and Levi had hardly slept. Their lovemaking had been sweet and tender at first. He had taken his time, finding ways to bring her pleasure. As if he were trying to convince her that he was worthy of her. But afterward, they found a new fierceness between them. She couldn't get enough of his hands on her body or the taste of him on her tongue. They had been rough and hurried. Heat filled her face as the memories played like an R-rated movie.

Skyla glanced at Bailey helping a customer, then hanging returned books with no covers on the Christmas tree as ornaments. Any more thoughts of Levi would have to wait.

She had to tell Bailey today about the DNA results burning a hole in her purse. She also wanted to tell Levi and couldn't put off the inevitable much longer. After Levi revealing what he had done to Grant, she couldn't keep her secret any longer. Secrets crushed everything in their path. Even if she lost her job at the bookstore, she would have the truth.

Skyla had read many articles online about families accepting newfound siblings. The articles didn't say whether or not that new sibling was homeless, sleeping in her car, an embarrassment. She couldn't, at the moment, undo the part where she lived in her car. But maybe with Levi's help, she finally would.

Skyla also had no idea what kind of a man Joe Russo was other than he loved his children and sea glass. If she tarnished Bailey and her sister's image of their father, they might not want her around anyway.

The door swung open and brought Colin in on the cold wind. The sun had come out today and brightened the sky into a vibrated blue.

"Hi, Colin." She waved.

He only put his hand up and ducked behind one of the stacks. She peered around the shelf to find him in the history section again. She approached him as if he were a scared kitten.

"Is there anything I can help you with?" She enjoyed helping the customers and Colin was a bit of a mystery to be solved.

He glanced at her, then away with a shake of his head. "I like to browse."

According to Bailey, he never purchased. Browsing books was a common enough occurrence in a bookstore. She would do that sometimes to get out of the cold or the oppressive heat. If the store allowed, she would even grab a book and find a place to sit and read. Books had saved her so many times in her life. They gave her a place to go when the real world hammered her over the head. She wondered if books did that for Colin too.

"What do you like to read?"

"History." He continued to keep his gaze on the books.

"Do you live in Serenity?"

"Would you mind if I looked in peace?"

She startled. "Sure. Sorry to bother you. Let me know if you need anything."

He only nodded.

She returned to a box of books behind the register with the weight of embarrassment on her shoulder. Bailey came up to her, then whispered in her ear, "I should have warned you. He doesn't like to talk. I usually leave him alone."

"It's very kind of you to allow him to browse for so long." Considering how rude he always seemed to be.

Bailey gave her a quizzical look. "Don't all bookstores do that?"

"Not all." She could think of a few where she had been run out of for staying too long and not buying. She always hoped that no one had noticed, but one time a manager had been keeping an eye on her, probably worried Skyla would steal something or hurt someone. He had come over and bellowed that she needed to leave or he would call the authorities. She had grabbed her backpack and run for the hills.

"Huh. I figured all bookstores were like ours." Bailey glanced at Colin again. "I don't think he has a lot of friends or family. If coming here gives him a few hours of enjoyment, I don't want to stop that."

"You're very generous."

"We all need a break once in a while. Thanks for taking care of the books. When you're done, could you look at the elf costumes for the kids' event? I want to finish with the tree."

"Sure thing. Great idea with the tree. At least those books will get some use."

"I hate to send them back to be destroyed." Bailey glued hooks onto another book to be hung.

"Are you worried about having a tree like that in the window? It might tempt this crazy arsonist running around town."

"I don't think this person will break into the store. We have cameras. Jack insisted we install them."

"How is Jack?"

"Same." Bailey pressed her lips into a thin line and gave a shrug. "How's Melvin doing?"

"Levi said he's pretty angry about the house and at the insurance company. I don't blame him. Standing there helpless when his house was on fire froze me to the spot. I can't imagine how he feels, losing his home." Actually, she could. She had been evicted from her apartment with nowhere to live. Fear had stalked her around every dark corner.

"Who knows what would have happened if Melvin had been home?" Bailey said.

"Lucky for him he wasn't." Colin had snuck up on them without a sound. "Or he'd be toast." A flicker of a smile crossed his pale lips.

The door swung open again. Captain Wright from the fire department stalked into the store. He gave a hearty wave. "Afternoon. I'm looking for a book by Lisa Olech. It's for my sister for Christmas."

"I can help you with that. I just opened a box with her books in it." She reached for the nearby box and pulled out *Fire Casts No Shadow*, the author's new release. She handed a copy to Captain Wright.

"Any word on the arsonist?" Colin asked Captain Wright.

"Everyone was in the bakery this morning talking about the fire still," Bailey said.

"No word yet, but a good thing Skyla here and Levi were home to call for help."

"I'd never thought I'd say this but thank the Universe that Levi had bought that house. Otherwise, no one would have been on that street. That middle home has been empty for a decade. Melvin's home would have burned to the ground." Bailey shivered and rubbed her arms.

"I heard some whispering. I was at the bakery this morning too," Colin said.

"I'll take the book," Captain Wright said.

"I hadn't known anyone else lived on River Road. I wonder if the arsonist does." Colin twisted the strap to the bag he had slung over his shoulder.

"What does that mean?" She searched Colin's face for some answer, but he offered none. His dark eyes were blank.

Captain Wright turned and regarded Colin too. "Interesting question, son. I was thinking the same thing. Those houses have been neglected. I thought old Melvin had moved out by now. Three empty houses is a mighty fine place to start a fire."

"But they aren't empty." Skyla rung up the book sale for the captain.

"Did the person setting the fire know that?" Bailey's gaze moved around the circle of people. "Were they trying to do more harm than just a fire?"

"Sometimes. You all be careful." Captain Wright took his purchase and left.

"You and Levi have to be extra cautious. Lots of trees across the street too." Colin licked his lips.

"Did you find anything you wanted today?" Bailey asked Colin and Skyla was grateful for the change in subject. Colin's presence set her nerves on end. He may be a lonely man, but something about him rubbed her wrong.

"No, thank you. I'm leaving now. Goodbye."

As the door closed on his departure, Bailey turned to her. "I don't think he meant to scare you with his comment about the trees."

She did. "Would the arsonist set the whole park on fire? What is this guy after?"

"I hope whoever it is has stopped. Many years ago, someone started a fire in the Pine Barrens with a cigarette.

The fire burned ten thousand acres. A fire in that park would destroy the whole park."

"And our homes." Flames could leap across the street from the park and devour the houses in one swoop. She and Levi needed to be vigilant.

"Where in town does Colin live?" She went back to unpacking books and checking them in to inventory.

"No one likes to talk about it, but Serenity has a boarding house on the edge of town. Big, beautiful Victorian that was once a vacation home for an oil tycoon in the eighteen hundreds. Someone along the way renovated it. The rent is cheap. It's clean. But it does attract transients. Not great for the tourist season or young families wanting the good schools."

"And that's where Colin lives?" A room in a big old Victorian house would be paradise. At least until she got on her feet and could rent something bigger. A room to herself behind a locked door no one could barge through would give back her freedom and independence. She couldn't stay with Levi forever. He was gracious to share as much as he had, but she needed to make her own way again. She wanted to be in a relationship with him as a woman who could take care of herself. Who had a life worth sharing.

"Yup. The house manager keeps an eye on him."

Skyla mustered up the nerve to broach the topic she had avoided until now. "Do you have some time later to talk? There's something I want to discuss with you."

The words hung in the air out of reach enough that she couldn't pull them back. She had wanted this path. Had found Serenity by the Sea on a map and driven over a hundred miles to come here with one goal. Everything else that had happened while she was in town was gravy.

"Why don't you tell me now? The store is quiet at the moment, and I want to leave on time. Tonight's the Christmas Under the Stars event. I'm meeting my sister Kassidy there. Are you going?"

"I didn't know anything about it."

"It's a lot of fun. Vendors set up tables. Food trucks come. There's a band playing Christmas songs. The Winter Wrappers. There are games. You should come."

"Maybe."

"I keep interrupting you. I'm sorry. What did you want to talk to me about?"

The words in her head, words she had rehearsed, dried up on her tongue. She wasn't prepared for this speech; she needed more time. What seemed like a good idea a minute ago could turn into the biggest mistake of her life.

Whenever something had been in her reach and she grabbed for it, life took it away from her. She had lost her mother too soon. Then she had found a man who loved her, and they had made a child, but Skyla hadn't been allowed to keep either person. The life she had worked for had been stolen from her.

Now she had another chance at some happiness. She had a job here and one with Levi. Levi had been an unex-pected surprise that had swooped in and stolen her heart. Made her realize that what she had with Will had never been real. Levi would not abandon her when her chips were down. He was in her corner.

If she told Bailey they were sisters, would life snatch

away this chance for happiness too and take every gift that had fallen into her lap? She wouldn't risk it. She could live with being a coworker, maybe a friend. She didn't need sisters.

"Skyla, are you okay? Your face went white."

She could never hide her feelings even when she thought she had done a good job of keeping emotion off her face. She would have to hope her voice held a strength she didn't have.

"Is it warm in here? I'm not feeling so good all of a sudden. I hope I'm not getting sick. Maybe I'll just go splash some cold water on my face." A lame excuse, but if she hid in the bathroom long enough, Bailey might forget Skyla wanted to talk to her about anything.

The door swung open again, bringing another welcomed distraction. Maren barreled into the store carrying several shopping bags and an exasperated look.

"Oh, good. You're still here. Are you coming to Christmas Under the Stars tonight?" Maren looked her way without much more than a glance. "Hello, Skyla."

"Hi, Maren."

"Of course I am. Who would miss that?"

"Sea Glass is supposed to have a tent. Hank is making hamburgers, hot dogs, and sloppy joes. Except he can't now. He's got to cover at the restaurant. Can you help out?"

"Do you mean Sea Glass, the restaurant?" Her research on Bailey had dropped her on a website for a restaurant owned by the three sisters that was once owned by their father. Skyla would love to hear more about the old tavern and what it was like to be a kid there.

Maren narrowed her eyes. "How long have you been in town?"

"Not long." She had given herself away. How would she know about the restaurant if she just came to town? It wasn't summer season. Most of the businesses were closed for the winter. Sea Glass wasn't. But Maren didn't know what Skyla knew or didn't.

"I like to drive around a new town until I get my feel for the streets. I passed it the other day." Not a total lie. She drove around lots of towns, killing time or trying to find day work.

"You should have lunch there," Bailey said. "You'll love it."

"I'll do that." When she had disposable income. She might even take Levi there on a real date someday.

"Anyway," Maren steered the conversation back with an eye roll, "Kassidy and I are going to handle the food, but I can't do it the whole time. I promised Shane I would help out at the university's tent. Some of the athletes are dressing up like reindeer and handing out toys to the kids. Could you help the second half of the night?"

"Just not during The Winter Wrappers' performance."

"That's fine. They're going on early. Also, can Jack babysit Emma for a little while? Grant offered to play a set with Kenny's band before he knew we were shorthanded." Maren glanced at Skyla again, but her rigid posture said everything Maren didn't.

Maren didn't want her around. But Skyla would not be deterred. She wanted to know who Kenny was, and if Grant was playing in what sounded like a performance, Levi might want to come and see. She needed more information before being chased away like an errant child.

"Jack is taking Luther to his mom's tonight. Ever since Luther moved in with us, Sloane has been calling all the time to arrange visits. She hasn't adjusted to the new arrangement well and Jack doesn't want her to feel badly during the holidays. He usually hangs out in a coffee shop if Luther isn't spending the night. Which he isn't this time. He doesn't want to miss the party at school tomorrow," Bailey said.

Skyla stored away the information that Jack had a young son. Her heart ached to hold her own child. Sometimes being around other people's children broke open the hole inside her and mending it again took a needle and thread she didn't have. Right after Emory, Skyla couldn't be around anyone else's children. She had lost all her friends who were raising kids because she stopped answering their calls. No one understood the pain and for some, what had happened to her might be contagious. They didn't want to risk ending up like her.

"I understand. I asked Peyton but she's got finals and doesn't have the time to break away. Who else can we ask?" Maren tapped her finger to her lip.

"Skyla, could you watch Emma for an hour or two? She's an easy baby."

"Oh, I don't know." Panic banged around inside her head. She wasn't ready to smell the sweet scent of an infant or touch the softest skin. No. No. No.

"Kassidy won't let her fifteen-month-old stay with anyone she hasn't fingerprinted," Maren said.

"That settles it, then. I'll let you two talk. Excuse me, nature calls." She needed to slip away before she went into a full-blown panic attack.

"Skyla, hang on," Bailey said. "You could keep an eye on Emma right by the Sea Glass tent. You'd just be an extra pair of hands and Kassidy could see you with the baby."

"Bailey, what are you doing?" Maren's voice held venom.

"I really need to go to the bathroom. I'll be right back." Skyla stopped at the top of the hall that led to the bathroom. She pressed against the wall, out of sight, to hear if they continued to talk about her.

"I get a bad vibe from her, Bailey. What were you thinking, asking her to babysit? She's a complete stranger." If Maren had tried to whisper, she had failed.

"Shh. Keep your voice down. I don't want her to hear you say not nice things about her."

At least Bailey had come to her defense, but it appeared Skyla was right about Maren.

"We don't know her."

"She's fine. You're being overprotective like usual. I think she's lonely."

"What makes you think that?"

"She came to town with Levi Hawkins, for one. She's new here. And even though she claims she works for Levi, why does she want to work here too? Levi can't be good company."

"He might not be the best company for Skyla. I get it, but she can't babysit for Emma. Kassidy and Grant won't allow it," Maren said.

"Okay, fine. You're probably right. I shouldn't have said anything without talking to Kassidy first. Don't tell her, okay?"

Maren laughed. The first joyful sound Skyla noticed coming from the woman. But she should be fair. Skyla was a stranger, and Maren was watching out for her family.

"Your secret is safe with me. I have to run. We'll figure out the babysitting part. I'll see you later," Maren said, slamming Skyla back to the present.

"Love you."

"Love you too."

Skyla held her breath, then slipped into the bathroom before Bailey noticed her. The small room was for one and she locked the door and leaned against it to still her heart. The bathroom was clean with its white walls and pedestal sink. If someone sat on the toilet, they could probably wash their hands at the same time. She liked it. Just like everything else about this bookstore and its owner. Skyla was in over her head.

She splashed cold water on her face and dried up with some paper towels. She would not be accepted by Maren. Skyla didn't want to make life difficult for Bailey by telling her and her sisters that their father had been unfaithful. She wouldn't tell and that was final. No more back and forth.

Some secrets were better kept buried.

When she returned to the front of the store, Maren was gone. Bailey handed a female customer with dark hair and a warm smile her purchase in a brown paper bag.

"Merry Christmas," Bailey said.

"Same to you." The customer left.

Bailey turned to her. "That's Sunny Copeland. She's a local author. She's very supportive of our store. I adore her. I'll introduce you next time."

"That would be nice. If you're okay, I have some errands to run."

"I'm sorry about the whole babysitting thing. Please forgive my sister's behavior before."

"Not to worry. She was fine."

"No, she was rude. She's overprotective of us and it takes her a while to warm up, but when she does, Maren is the best person to have in your corner. She'd do anything for her family."

"That's nice." Would someone like Maren have helped her before she landed on the street? Skyla liked to think so.

"Will you come to the Christmas Under the Stars with me?"

"Oh, no. I can't. I don't want to intrude." She also didn't want Maren giving her the death glare all evening. Skyla preferred to head back to the cottage after eavesdropping on Maren and Bailey.

"Please come. It's so much fun. You'll love The Winter Wrappers. There's a tree decorating contest and hot chocolate. They do a scavenger hunt. Since you're new in town, I could introduce you to a few people, including my sister Kassidy and her husband Grant. Wait. Have you met Grant?"

"I have but only recently." From her two encounters, Grant seemed like the difficult brother. If she had her chance, she would tell Grant he was being a fool to stay mad at Levi.

"Grant's a really good guy. I hope Levi is telling you that."

"Levi only has nice things to say about Grant."

"That's good to hear. Do you have any siblings?" Bailey placed a star on top of her book tree.

Skyla considered again what life would be like if she told the truth. She was as certain now as she was wiping her hands in that pristine bathroom that no good would come out of telling the truth. Though a small part of her would have liked to know her father's side of the story. Would he have been the kind of man who would have been glad to have Skyla in his life, or would he have shunned her because he already had three daughters?

She met Bailey's gaze more determined than ever to do the right thing for herself.

"No siblings. I'm an only child."

Chapter Twenty

"You're putting this high-end furniture in here?" Melvin turned in circles in Levi's living room. "This house isn't the place for things like leather sofas so soft against my rough hands that they feel like butter. I wouldn't want to put my backside clothed in my Sunday best on those things for fear of dirtying them up."

"They weren't that expensive." He wouldn't tell Melvin how much he had spent. He hadn't the time to shop all over the place, so he called his interior designer from his last house and asked her to find some simple things he could put in this fixer-upper.

He wanted Skyla's opinion about how to arrange the furniture, but she wasn't back yet from the bookstore. He wished she wouldn't work there. If the Russo sisters convinced her that he was no good, she might believe them. It would be four against one, including Grant. Levi might not stand a chance against that.

He reminded himself of the way she was with him last

night. His broken body hadn't scared her away. She had barely paid attention to his loss. Another woman, a woman who wanted him because of his wealth, might have turned and ran. But Skyla didn't seem to care about his money, always busting him for having it. There was a woman who needed money and kept turning his down.

"You should've painted first, son." Melvin's words tore him away from thoughts of last night and Skyla's body responding to his.

"I don't think I thought this all the way through." And he hadn't. He wanted something to sit on and sleep on and eat at. His back hurt from lying on that inflatable mattress even if Skyla was in his arms.

"You better hire Darrel the painter. I'll get you his number. He's reasonable and reliable. Two things that are hard to find in a painter. He'll come with his drop cloths. He'll make it right."

"Thanks. Any word on who started the fire?" He moved the sofa to the one wall that didn't have a window.

"You're sticking out into the hallway over here." Melvin helped him try the corner next. "The fire department says it's too soon to say who started the fire. They're comparing notes on the others, looking for patterns and whatnot."

"Investigating takes time." He didn't like the sofa in the corner and tried it under the window. From there he could still watch the fireplace and maybe a television if he decided to hang one.

"Whoever did it probably walked right in the front door. I don't lock it when I'm not home. Just at night when I go to sleep and take out my hearing aids. I don't understand why this fella picked me." Melvin's shoulders sagged as if pushed by the weight of the incident.

"Do you have any problems with anyone in town?" He moved the coffee table in front of the sofa and then the one matching chair to the short side of the table. "This might be the best spot for them."

"Fills in the room and lets you talk to people in the dining room if you're planning on having guests."

"Not really." He wouldn't be inviting anyone from his old life to come out here. They would want to know why Levi would sell his large home and move into something that he could cross in three strides. They didn't understand why he left the business either, but he hadn't told anyone about the cancer or the treatment. That battle he fought on his own and when he had won, he had decided life needed to be simpler in all ways. Objects didn't matter as much as he had thought.

"Like I told the police, if someone in this town has a problem with me, I don't know about it. Delivered mail for thirty-five years on Serenity's streets. Used to know everyone too by face and house number. I didn't like every-one, believe me, but I kept my opinions to myself. When you have to walk onto someone's porch each day and drop their mail in their box, you don't want to cause trouble with them. Used to keep treats in my sack for the dogs too."

"Maybe picking the trees is random." He glanced out the window. The sky was blue today. Snow had covered the branches of the trees across the street like a white blanket, but in the sun's warmth, that blanket melted in spots.

Would those trees be next to catch fire? Would that

person come back here and try to set the houses on fire? With Melvin gone, he and Skyla were alone out here, away from town. He wished he had a gun to protect them if anyone showed up in the middle of the night with crazy ideas.

"I suppose choosing whose tree goes up could be random. Doesn't matter much now. My house is destroyed. It's going to take months, maybe a year, to fix it up. I might just walk away and let the insurance company have it. I could go live with my cousin in Vermont."

"You're a damn good neighbor, Melvin. I'd hate to lose you." He took the hallway to the master bedroom and beckoned Melvin to follow. Levi wanted the bed made before Skyla returned from work.

He had told the delivery guys to put the bed frame on the wall opposite the windows so they could see the sun come up over the river in the morning. Thinking as if Skyla would sleep in his bed night after night could get him in a world of hurt. She had a lot of baggage to unpack and so did he. But she fit him in ways he didn't understand and didn't need to for now.

"Ah. You've been here all of five minutes. I might be a terrible neighbor." Melvin took one end of the sheet and tucked it around the corner of the mattress while he did the same on his side.

"That's why you brought over beer when I moved in and today you came with bread and cheese." Melvin had arrived the same time today as the furniture truck. He had helped Levi direct the delivery drivers. Levi had appreciated the help. He would've liked to have Grant with him, like in the old days, but he didn't want to push his luck at the moment. Grant had stopped by after the fire at Melvin's. It was a start.

"You don't go to anyone's house empty-handed. Didn't your mother teach you that?"

"She did, in fact. She would say to me and my brothers, 'Now, boys, I didn't raise you to be animals. When you call on someone or accept their invite, you show up with a pound cake or some cookies at least. If you don't have time to bake, flowers for the missus and a bottle of bourbon for the mister. But those hands of yours will not be empty.'"

"Wise woman, your mother. Do you see her much?" Melvin shoved a pillow into the case.

"I wish. She's been gone since I was a teenager." He tossed a new blanket on the bed too. That old ratty one Skyla dragged around as if she were a modern-day Linus needed a date with the trash.

"Sorry to hear that. How about those brothers? You spend time with them?"

"My brother Emmett died in an accident several years back." He didn't mind talking about Emmett. He took every chance he could, unlike Grant.

The other bedrooms would remain empty for now unless Skyla wanted to sleep in one of them instead of with him. He hoped she wouldn't switch rooms.

The house still needed plenty of work which he would do by himself or with contractors he hired. He wasn't going to pay Skyla any longer to work for him.

"Damn, son. You've had some heartache."

"We all have." Skyla had the kind of pain that would

break the strongest soul in two. She had lost a child. He could only imagine the pain to be equal to touching the fiery surface of the sun.

"Even if others have their share of bad luck, doesn't make our suffering any less. I'm sorry about your family. I lost my brother in Vietnam. Miss him every day."

"Sorry to hear that too." He went back into the living room. Not much else to do until Skyla returned.

"What about the other brothers? How many you have anyway?"

"Three of us in total. You might know my oldest brother. Grant Hawkins."

Melvin stopped in his tracks. "The one married to Kassidy Russo? Plays at Sea Glass some nights. He was a big rock star once, wasn't he?"

"He doesn't like to be reminded." Especially not after he found out that Levi had written songs in Grant's name.

"Then you came to town to live near him."

"I didn't think that idea all the way through either." He was grateful Grant had shown up to check on him, but his stubborn brother wouldn't let go of his grudge no matter how many times Levi apologized. He had done what he did with those songs for Grant as much as for himself. At least that was what he thought at the time. No one got hurt. Grant made money. He had made money too. Everyone won, but Grant had wanted his head.

"Sounds like family trouble."

"You're perceptive, Melvin." He flopped onto the couch. The old story of fighting siblings and rearranging furniture wore him out. His back ached again.

Melvin took the matching chair.

"Do you need to get something off your chest, son?"

"Why would you say that?"

"The look in your eyes. I've seen it before in men who carry a burden they don't want to share because they think either no one cares or a real man would tough it out."

"I've done some things I'm not proud of. Grant reminds me every time he sees me that I'm a screwup."

"Was Skyla his girl before he met Kassidy?" Melvin arched a wiry brow.

"Nothing like that. Business stuff I can't undo." Didn't want to undo either.

"Can you make it right?"

"He won't accept my apology."

"He doesn't have to. You just keep doing it. If he's important to you and you want him in your life, that is. You keep knocking on his door until you break through to him."

"What if I can't?"

"At least you die trying." Melvin pushed out of his seat. "I'm heading back now. It's been a long day, and these old bones want to sit in front of the fire and sip some whiskey while the Christmas music plays."

Levi walked him to the door.

"Nice touch with the Christmas tree in the backyard. Did you do that for Skyla?"

"I did. But I didn't want it in the house."

"Smart. Everyone is a suspect, you know. You watch your back. And if I don't see you before, Merry Christmas."

"You're coming back to River Road. We need you."

"Don't know what the future holds. I'll be in touch."

"Merry Christmas, Melvin."

Levi stood on the porch until Melvin's car turned the corner out of sight. The sun seemed in a bigger hurry today to hand over his work to the moon or Levi hadn't realized how long he and Melvin had been at it this afternoon. The wind kicked in again, not ready to release its hold on the weather, and ran its cold fingers over Levi's skin.

Shadows spread across the street between the trees lining the road. River Road was secluded. Anyone could come through those trees from the park just like Skyla had when he first met her. That was probably how the arsonist got to Melvin's house. How alone were they? Or was someone watching now?

No sign of Skyla on the silent street. Levi returned indoors. Melvin had been right. That sofa and chair don't belong in this house. He'd ask Skyla for her opinion when she returned and let her pick out something she liked better. He wanted her touch in every room.

He wished she had returned already.

Chapter Twenty-One

Skyla hesitated on the front porch. Night sucked the day into its darkness, leaving behind nothing but gray skies between the branches of the barren trees in the park and above the river. The air smelled of snow again. Nothing might come of another fall. Winter by the ocean didn't often develop inches of snow, but this had been the strangest December for her. Why shouldn't snow fall?

Lights burned inside the house, lighting up the windows in a lemon-yellow glow. The furniture had arrived, and Levi must have set up the living room. Woodsmoke curled out of the fireplace and added its perfume to the air.

After she had left the bookstore, she had driven around for a while. She took a pass by Sea Glass and imagined what her father might have been like. She had always had a piece of herself missing from the whole. A piece she could not find until she realized who her biological father was. Now, fear kept her from ruining the first friendship she had developed in a long time. Loneliness had clung to her like a wet wool blanket in the same way being homeless had. She was tired of dragging around the dampness. She wanted to be free of it. And Bailey had handed her a chance by thinking Skyla was good enough to babysit her niece.

She wanted Levi to attend the event tonight with her. Going alone turned her insides to icicles. Maren did not want her around Bailey. In enough time, Bailey might be convinced. Even if Levi wasn't their favorite person, he was confident and that strength seeped into her.

The door opened before she could put her hand on the knob.

"What are you doing standing on the porch?" Levi stood before her in a blue flannel shirt, jeans, and thick socks. The woodsmoke smell followed him outside onto the porch.

"I was just about to come in."

He placed a kiss on her frigid lips and moved aside to allow her to pass. The living room was warm from the blazing fire and swallowed up the new furniture. The pieces dwarfed the room and seemed out of place in the tired cabin, but she didn't want to hurt Levi's feelings by saying so.

"Where have you been all day?" He retrieved an open beer from the coffee table.

She regarded him and his question. He could mean nothing more than simple curiosity or his message could have a deeper meaning. One she may not like, but Levi had never been possessive. Not that he had a reason to be. They were too new for that.

"I spent most of the day at the bookstore. I told you I was working today."

"I didn't mean to sound... I missed you. Melvin is good company, but he's not you."

She hung her coat on the hook by the door and dropped her bag on the table by the window. "I'll take that as a compliment."

"You should."

"After work, I went for a drive. Needed to think. The furniture looks nice."

"It's too much for this cabin. I might return it. What's on your mind?"

She moved into the kitchen. "Are you hungry? I could fix us something."

Levi followed her, then gripped her wrist. "Is something wrong?"

"What makes you say that?" She eased away. Nothing was wrong except her nerves had the best of her again. She and Levi had slept together more than once and still she couldn't form the words to ask him to go with her tonight.

"You seem a little jumpy. I'm sorry if I sounded like a possessive asshole a minute ago."

"I'm the one who should be sorry. I'm overreacting to something."

"Can I help?"

She smoothed her sweaty palms over her shirt. "Would you like to go on a date with me?"

His smile took a stroll across his chiseled face. "Yes, ma'am, I would indeed."

"Great. I'd like to take you to the Christmas Under the

Lights event tonight in town." She had a few dollars from his payment to her for the work she'd done. Though she had hardly done anything at all. She could splurge on a hot chocolate for them.

"That big thing that's set up over by the theater?"

"I believe that's where it is, yes. Would you like to go?"

His smile slipped. "I really want to spend time with you. But I don't want to go to a big town event. Grant will most likely be there. If he sees me, we'll just end up arguing. I'm not up for that tonight. What if we find a movie theater out of town? My treat."

She rearranged her face to hide the disappointment. "Grant is playing tonight with someone named Kenny."

"Don't know who that is."

"Well, anyway, I thought maybe you could join them."

"Play with my brother?" Levi hooted with laughter. "Grant would rather I drown in the ocean than play with me again. Thanks, but I'll pass."

"He doesn't want you to die. He's mad, but he'll get over it."

"You don't know Grant. Besides, I don't want to get up onstage with him. Our days playing together are over. I don't even want to play by myself."

"It was just an idea." She busied herself with a can of soup and the can opener that wouldn't cooperate.

Levi slid the tool from her hand. "Before you cut open something other than this can. I appreciate you trying. I do. But Grant has to come to me when he's ready. And I'm not ready to see him in town in front of all the people he's been living with for the past several years. He's one of them now. I'm the outsider."

"If we go together, we can be a team of outsiders."

"You're already fitting in. You have a job. You're making friends with Bailey. I think that's great. I'm going to stay home, but you go."

"You want me to go by myself?" She needed him there. Maren had intimidated her. With Levi by her side, she could pull from his strength.

"I want you to do whatever you want to do. Stay. Go. It's up to you. We can go on a date another night." He flopped down on the sofa and pulled out his phone.

The conversation must be over, and she was no longer hungry. Heat burned her cheeks again. This time not from the memory of their lovemaking, but of being foolish enough to put her heart out there and have it handed back to her.

"There's a boarding house on the edge of town. Did you know that?"

"Nope." He didn't glance up from his phone.

"Levi, why are you ignoring me? A minute ago, you seemed glad to see me. Now you can't be bothered." She was looking for a fight, and she didn't know why.

He dragged his gaze away from his screen. "I don't understand why you would suggest I try to get Grant to allow me onstage with him after I told you the whole story between him and me."

"It was just an idea."

"It was a dumb idea."

"You know what? I don't have to take this from you. I never asked you for anything. You gave me a place to stay, a bed to sleep in, and food because you chose to. I guess you must've really felt sorry for the homeless girl who lost her child."

He stood. "You don't believe that, do you?"

"I said it, didn't I?" She held his gaze.

"Skyla, come on. Why are you fighting with me?"

Exhaustion owned her. Maren didn't like her, thought she was up to no good. People in this town whispered that she might be the arsonist. She was afraid the actual arsonist would hurt them. And she was afraid of the way she cared for Levi.

"Was I your charity case? And now that I'm trying to stand on my own two feet, you want to keep me down by pushing me away."

"I've been nothing but good to you. I've never judged you or asked anything of you. I just don't want to go into town tonight and get my head handed to me by my brother."

"Not even for me?"

"Ask for anything else. Anything."

"I don't want anything else. You might as well know that as soon as I can, I'm going to rent a room at that boarding house."

"You don't want to live here?"

"I need to find my independence again."

"Are you ending things between us?"

She hadn't planned on it. She had planned on starting a real life with him. But standing in this cottage still in so much need of repair, filled with furniture that didn't belong, she was the house. She had so much left to heal. She didn't fit here with Levi. She needed to find her way.

"I don't know."

"Please, Skyla. Don't do this. Not because I'd rather stay home."

"You have to deal with your brother at some point."

"I've been trying."

"Try again. Find the thing that will convince him. Because you have to ask yourself, what are you afraid of?"

"Can't I ask the same of you? What are you running from here? It's not that I won't go out with you. It's bigger than that."

Fear wrapped itself around her neck and pulled. The room was too warm. She needed fresh air and a chance to think. She had juggled more than she could handle these last years and now everything crashed around her. Maybe it was because these last weeks moved at breakneck speed. Maybe because her heart had led her down a path she didn't know how to get off. She couldn't turn around and she couldn't go forward. Not with the truth. The truth of who she was. The truth about her feelings for Levi. The truth that she was still clawing her way out of her mess. The truth that she had no right to be happy if her child was not walking the earth.

"I'm handling my problems. You handle yours. I'm going to the Christmas event. Stay here. I don't want you to come anyway. Tomorrow I'll find another place to live."

"Skyla, please don't say that."

She turned and hurried from the house because if she stayed a second longer and witnessed the pain flash through his dark eyes, she would do something stupid like tell him she loved him.

Chapter Twenty-Two

"What the hell just happened?" Levi said to no one and stared at the spot Skyla stood a moment ago.

The glow of her headlights passed through the window like a lighthouse beacon. Except she wasn't lighting the way to anything. She had left him in the dark.

He didn't understand her change of heart toward him. Last night, while he held her in his arms, her body still slick with sweat from their lovemaking, he had been certain she felt for him the way he did for her. His heart had expanded until it threatened to burst free. He wanted to protect her and support her and love her. He had almost said it again but stopped himself at the last second, worried that he would scare her.

He was glad he hadn't repeated those words now. He paced the space by the window, having little room to move because of the oversized sofa. He kicked the leg. He didn't understand if she wanted to break it off with him or not.

If she wanted to go, he would have no choice. But he

wanted a chance to convince her to stay. He should have said he'd go with her, but he didn't want to see Grant again. And she always believed anything could be fixed if she tried. He had no idea how she stayed positive after all she'd been through. He couldn't get out of bed for weeks after his diagnosis. He hadn't wanted to live and here she was swinging for the fences. And wow. She liked baseball. He was a sucker for this woman.

But suggesting he play with Grant was absurd. He shouldn't have laughed at her. He would apologize for that. He had to make her see he needed her. Not as a charity case. As his partner. For the first time in a long time, he was alive with her around.

He turned on his heel and knocked her bag to the ground. It toppled on its side. The contents spilled out as if he'd broken open a pinata.

He didn't inspect her items. Some couldn't be helped but noticed. Old makeup. Tissues. Pens. Coins that must've made their way to the bottom. Small notebooks. He wouldn't look in those. Her wallet. And a folded piece of paper that appeared official. A seal of some kind indented the back of the paper and would be raised on the other side.

He knew better than to spy and break a trust. She was already one foot out the door, but he was curious about the parts of her she kept hidden. She had shared so much with him already, but she held more secrets close to her.

He should allow her to tell him, if she wanted to, but she might never want to because she was afraid that he would change his mind about his feelings. He would never change his mind even if she did leave him.

He would not open her wallet, but this loose piece of paper couldn't be too important if it was only shoved into her bag and not tucked into a notebook. Before he could talk himself out of what he was about to do, he unfolded it.

The words blurred as he read. She had taken a DNA test as part of a study. The letter stated a check was included, but he guessed that was long gone. The results were below.

He scanned the page. She had a match. A half sister. Named Bailey Russo.

He dropped the page. Skyla had played him. Probably right from the first moment he walked up on her asleep in his house. House sales were public information. A few clicks and she would be able to figure out who owned it and with a few extra clicks, if someone was determined enough, they could connect the dots. Bailey and Kassidy were sisters. Kassidy was married to Levi's semi-famous brother. And that left him the fool once again.

Skyla had to park a quarter mile away. It might have been easier to walk over from River Road. But it was cold, and the sky still threatened snow. Now she walked the seven blocks back to the theater area where the Christmas Under the Stars event was underway.

Almost all the houses along the way were decorated for Christmas. One house displayed twenty inflatable Christmas characters that swayed in the wind as if waving to her as she passed. But their sweet smiles did nothing to lighten her mood.

She hunkered into her coat. Levi's refusal to come with her had hit harder than a rogue wave. She hadn't expected her insides to seize when he rejected her suggestion. Her knee-jerk reaction to the fear of being alone had caused her to start a fight with him. She had behaved like a child and would need to apologize. But she had put the end of their relationship in motion and maybe it was better if she did leave.

Christmas music drifted toward her as she turned onto Coastal Road. A band played up ahead. People filled the street and spilled all over the lawn in front of the theater.

Vendors lined the streets with their Christmas wares. The smell of roasted chestnuts filled the air. A bitter wind snuck in and penetrated her thin coat. The cold ate at her bones. What was she doing at something designed for friends and families? She had neither and now she might not have Levi because of her big mouth.

She searched for the Sea Glass tent and found it at the end of Serenity Street. Maren smiled and spoke with customers as she handed over food and drink purchases. A man wearing a bandana around his head moved around the grill with ease.

Skyla didn't see Kassidy or Bailey. She would wander around a bit and come back later. If Bailey wasn't there on the next pass through, Skyla would return to Levi's for the night. In the morning, she would inquire about a room at the boarding house.

Someone tapped her on the shoulder. She spun around,

hoping to see Levi. Instead, Bailey beamed at her from under her furry white hood.

"You made it. I'm so glad."

"I didn't think I'd find you in the crowd." The crowd expanded as if someone had blown out a large breath.

"It's great. Isn't it? I love this event. The whole town comes together. Where's Levi? I thought he might show up."

"Not interested."

"Men. Let's go have some fun." Bailey slipped her arm through Skyla's.

They navigated the crowd and bought caramel-covered apples on sticks. They ate while they walked from tent to tent admiring the beautiful things. Bailey didn't purchase anything and that allowed Skyla to breathe a little relief. She could admire, but there was no touching.

They ended up back at the makeshift stage where Grant and who Skyla would guess is Kenny had set up their equipment.

"What does Grant like to play?"

Bailey narrowed her eyes. "You don't know who Grant is?"

"Sure, I do. But didn't he leave the business?" She had paid no attention to pop culture of any kind after Emory was born. When they had received her diagnosis, the only thing Skyla had paid attention to was searching for a cure for her baby. Music had never crossed her mind. But she did know who Grant Hawkins was. He was Levi's older brother who didn't believe in forgiveness and didn't know how lucky he was to have a brother who loved him enough to change his life for Grant's forgiveness.

"Grant was huge until a bus accident some years back. He plays rock mostly. Hard and soft. Some blues."

"Levi did mention that. I forgot." She scanned the crowd for any sign of Levi, needing to talk to him, to make things right between them. She didn't want their relationship to end.

"Skyla, are you okay? You seem out of it." Bailey placed a gloved hand on her shoulder.

"Sure. Sure. Too much sugar." She tried to laugh the comment off, but Bailey regarded her with a look of suspicion.

Grant and Kenny began their first song, removing any more chances for discussion. Skyla enjoyed the music, but her mind wandered. No one could have it all. She believed that in her soul.

She came to this town with one goal—to find her sister and reveal herself. But she had become sidelined by feelings for a man she hadn't expected to meet and by a job she hadn't thought possible to have.

The job and the man were the trade-offs for a real family. Something she may never have had except for the few short years with her daughter. Some might say Levi could be her family. And he could, but didn't she deserve to be a part of the people she was born to or was that too much to ask?

She had to choose.

She wasn't sure if she could watch from the sidelines when she knew who her sisters were as they shared inside jokes and confidences. But she hadn't wanted them to be turned off by her circumstances and Maren was. Skyla went round and round until her head spun.

A hand gripped her shoulder and turned her around. Her feet slipped out from under her. She waited for the ground to connect with her butt, but the strong hand righted her.

She opened her mouth to yell at this inconsiderate person, but her words died on her lips.

Levi stood before her. He wore a black knit cap over his bald head. His parka hung open, revealing the flannel shirt underneath. His breath came out in white puffs.

"Hi, Levi," Bailey said.

He had come after all. She forced herself not to leap into his arms. He would have to make the first move in this sizeable crowd. Grant and Kenny played their next song.

Levi glanced at the stage, then back at her. That was the moment she realized he wasn't happy to see her. His dark eyes glared.

"What's the matter? Did the arsonist come back?" Had that maniac set fire to her lovely tree out by the river? Levi had been right to worry and she had insisted they have a tree. If the house suffered because of her, she would never forgive herself.

He shoved a piece of paper at her. Her brain hurried to catch up. Bailey stared on.

"You forgot your backpack." With his other hand, he shoved her sack at her. "I didn't mean to look, but I'm glad I did. You lied to me."

"You went through my things?"

"The paper fell out."

"You're not making sense." She tried to control her breathing and tell Levi with her eyes not to spill her story now. She needed more time. She would explain it all to him. But she had to be the one to tell Bailey or Skyla would lose all of it. Everything. Again.

"Come on, Skyla. We both know you used me to get to Bailey and her sisters."

"What? No."

"What's he saying?" Bailey stuck her head in closer.

"Nothing. Levi, can we talk about this later?"

"What's to talk about? You wanted a way to meet your sisters, and you used me to get it. You knew they wouldn't want anything to do with a homeless person."

"Homeless?" Bailey looked between the two of them.

"And they would be right to want nothing to do with you. What do you really want with any of us? Money? The restaurant? The bookstore? Did you think you were entitled to something because Joe Russo fathered another child he didn't want?"

"Skyla, what's he talking about?" Bailey looked at her with pain and confusion etched on her face.

"Tell her," Levi said.

"Not now." She had to make this right somehow.

"You're freaking me out. What's going on? Levi?" Bailey looked between the two of them again.

"We're sisters." She handed Bailey the DNA results.

Bailey glanced at them. "Why didn't you tell me?"

"Because she wants something from you," Levi said.

"That isn't true."

"All the time we spent together and not once you thought to mention it?" Bailey scanned the page again.

"Of course I did. I just couldn't find the right time, and then I didn't think it mattered."

"You thought it didn't matter? It doesn't matter that I have another sister? That my father once again had an affair that made a baby?" Bailey whipped her arms through the air.

"I'm sorry. I was afraid."

"Afraid of what? That we wouldn't like you or that we wouldn't welcome you into our family?"

"Probably the second because she was up to no good," Levi said.

She spun on her heel and locked gazes with Levi. "Shut up. You're making this worse. And you have it all wrong. I'm not using anyone. Neither one of you has any idea what it's like to be me or what I've been through." She pointed at Bailey. "If I showed up here and said, hi, I'm your half sister and I live in my car, what would you have said to me?"

Bailey opened her mouth but closed it again.

"I thought so."

"No, Skyla. Give me a chance to process all of this. I don't know what I would have said."

"I do. You would have said what everyone says when a homeless person comes near them. Get away."

"I would not."

"Whatever."

"I wish you had been honest. Hiding something like this makes you look underhanded. And I told you private things about Jack all while you kept your own big secret to yourself."

"I planned on telling you."

"When?"

"I don't know." She turned back to Levi. "Why are you so upset? My biology has nothing to do with you. I was honest with you about everything." She had trusted him with Emory's story.

"You left out a very important part. The part of why you came to this town. That you had a family that I was connected to, and you never told me. Skyla, we slept together."

"Oh, please. Don't you sit there and tell me every woman you slept with, you shared your most vulnerable self with."

"I didn't. But I did with you." He turned and walked away.

She called after him, but he kept going.

Bailey shook her head. "I don't know what your motivations were, if you were being honest or not. But right now, I can't trust you and Maren was right to be suspicious. I can't have you working in the store anymore. Skyla, you're fired."

Chapter Twenty-Three

Levi walked up one street and down the other. Anger kept him warm in the cold night. The sounds of the Christmas event had faded as he put miles on his shoes and hours between him and Skyla. He wished he could have stood around and listened to what Grant played these days, but he couldn't remain with her there.

He had wanted to believe what he and Skyla had shared was real. Sure, it had happened quicker than he thought possible, but some people fell in love at first sight and lasted a lifetime. Why couldn't that happen to him?

Because the woman he had fallen for had left out a very important part of her life. She could have told him at any point, but she had chosen to keep that secret. He didn't understand how she could share about the loss of her child, but not some stupid DNA test.

He didn't understand her motivation for lying to him. What was she after? Had she only wanted that damn business reference so she could work at the bookstore and manipulate Bailey? To what end?

His head pounded with all the thoughts of lies and deception. He was beyond that behavior now. He had wanted a clean slate. A second start. He didn't want to go back to an existence where lies for any reason were the answer. And Skyla had lied to him.

He passed the closed-up tents in the Topside Community. In the summer this area would be bustling. He stopped in front of the one he had rented for Grant the summer that things had changed for a second time. If he could go back, he would never have written those songs. Maybe he would have dodged cancer if he had been a better person. Was Skyla's deception part of the price for being a big a-hole his whole life?

He stepped off the corner and faced Grant's new house. The home originally belonged to Kassidy, but once she and Grant were married, they had renovated the bungalow into a two-story home. The smell of woodsmoke and women's laughter drifted toward him.

He walked up the side street and stopped near the privacy fence. He couldn't see through the slats, but Bailey and her sisters were probably sitting around a fire making s'mores. They had a lot to talk about tonight and sitting together in Kassidy's backyard was often how they hashed out their problems. Grant had told him that before they stopped speaking.

"How many more children did Dad have that we don't know about?"

"Bailey, check that ancestry site you sent your spit to and see if anyone else has popped up."

Levi wasn't entirely sure which sister had spoken, but it didn't matter. They all had a right to be upset about Skyla.

"Just Skyla. I wish I had checked sooner, but I did the test so long ago I forgot all about it. I unsubscribed from the emails and everything. I just wish she had told me."

"I told you I didn't like her."

"Maren, you don't like anyone."

Some laughter floated over the fence, and he took that as his cue to leave before Grant caught him eaves-dropping.

The ocean called to him. He crossed Ocean Ave and stood on the boardwalk in the wind caused by the massive body of water. Clouds covered the moon. Other than a few of the streetlights along the boardwalk, the beach was dark. The rhythm of the waves made their music even if Levi couldn't see the ocean all that well.

A light bounced along the sand, coming toward him. Someone was out there at the surf's edge, searching for something. A lot like him by coming to this town. He hoped whoever it was found what they were looking for because he hadn't.

He should consider selling the cottage. He couldn't stay in that house without Skyla in it. She was already in every room, her smell, her smile. He didn't want to be haunted by her memory.

He had no real reason to stay in town any longer. Grant had made himself clear even if he had shown up to check on him. Levi had been grasping at sand. He couldn't fix his relationship with his brother. Grant had to want things between them fixed too.

The bouncing light turned in his direction, then went out. A tall figure came out of the darkness into the dim glow set off by the streetlight. He would recognize that silhouette anywhere.

"What are you doing on my boardwalk?" Grant jogged up the steps and stood before him. He kicked his boots on the boards, probably to set free the sand in the grooves.

"You own the boardwalk too?" He flopped onto the bench. The weight of the day wore him out. He wasn't up for sparring with his brother.

"Hell of a day." Grant leaned against the railed metal fence and crossed his arms over his chest.

"Kassidy told you?"

"And Maren and Bailey all at the same time. Those Russo women cluck like a full henhouse. Thought my head would explode. I had to get out of there. Came down here to look for sea glass."

"You?"

"What can I say? Kassidy has rubbed off on me." Grant glanced down the street. "Did you know about Skyla being one of them?"

"Not a chance. She never said. Used me to get to Bailey."

"How do you figure that?"

"She wanted me for a reference so she could work at the bookstore. She had to know we were brothers and that you were married to Kassidy. Once she was on the inside, she could do whatever she had planned."

"Sounds like something out of a conspiracy novel."

"I don't know what her plan was. Maybe to get some of Joe's inheritance. Get close to the sister married to the famous musician. It doesn't matter." Skyla had used him. That was all that he knew. Whether she had wanted a way to Bailey or Kassidy or an inheritance that didn't exist, she had found her lapdog.

"Sounds like it matters plenty."

"Are you here to gloat? Because you can take a walk."

Grant pushed off the rail. "Not gloating, brother. Too old and too tired for that."

"Then what do you want?" He wanted Grant to walk away and leave him alone.

"Wanted to say it was too bad about Skyla. I could tell you cared about her."

"What gave you that idea?"

"You slouched on that bench and looking for a fight with me. Whenever a woman tangled you up, you came looking for a fight with me. Never Emmett."

"Emmett hit harder than you do." Levi had always looked to Grant for guidance when they were kids. Grant had watched out for him and Emmett. Didn't let anyone mess with them. Would step in the middle of many a fight. Grant had allowed him to be pissed at the world whenever he needed to and if that included Grant, he never stopped Levi from swinging.

"I should have had your back with the record label." He had said that a hundred times already, but he needed to say it again.

"That's right." Grant sat beside him.

"I'm sorry. If I could go back, I would."

"Yeah, well, I wasn't the easiest of clients back then." Grant's lip curled up in a half smile.

"Wow. Kassidy has rubbed off on you."

Grant kicked his foot. "Shut up."

"There's something you should know." The time had come to tell Grant about the cancer.

Fire engines screamed in the distance. He and Grant looked in the direction of the noise.

"The arsonist," Levi said. "They need to catch him before someone gets hurt."

"Hopefully no one gets hurt. Houses can be replaced."

"Even if there are no outside scars, someone is hurt." He thought of Melvin, losing his home of fifty years. That had to hurt even if Melvin didn't say it out loud.

"Who are you and what did you do with my brother?" Grant gave him a sideways glance.

"You're a prick."

"What is it you think I should know?"

He turned and looked his brother in the eye. "I had testicular cancer."

"Shit. Had? Is it gone?" Grant's body stiffened.

"Yeah. I'm good."

"Why didn't you tell me?" His brother relaxed against the back of the bench and looked out toward the water.

"Didn't want you forgiving me out of guilt."

"Guilt? Nah. I'd still be pissed at you. But I would've come to help you out. Who was there for you?"

"No one. I beat it by myself."

Grant blew out a long breath. "You are crazy. You didn't have to suffer alone."

"What's done is done. I handled it." He handled it the best he could at the time and had often wished for his brother to be by his side, but he had hurt Grant. Levi had no right to ask for help then.

"You're sure it's gone? You need anything?"

"It's gone. Took my left testicle with it." He was getting used to the idea. After being with Skyla, he didn't have to worry as much about what a woman thought. Skyla had accepted him.

When the right woman came along for real this time, she would understand. Skyla had at least been the right woman for the first time he had sex after the surgery. For that, he would be grateful.

The sirens grew louder. A pickup with a blue light on the dashboard sped down the road. Red lights flashed in the near distant sky.

"That's close," Levi said.

"Too close." Grant's phone rang. He pulled it out of his pocket. "It's Kassidy. I'll put her on speaker. Hey, babe. I'm here with Levi."

"Grant, the house is on fire."

Chapter Twenty-Four

Skyla packed the last of her things into the car. She had hurried back to Levi's after Bailey had made it clear Skyla wasn't wanted. Serenity offered her nothing now. She had lost Levi and the family she had coveted all because of fear.

Her behavior wasn't rational. Any rookie therapist could figure that out. But Skyla had lived the greater part of her life afraid. She had hoped Levi understood that, but he hadn't because he believed she had manipulated him. And maybe she had.

A total stranger had offered her a roof over her head and a warm bed to sleep in. She would have done just about anything to make that happen, including saying or doing just about whatever that stranger wanted. While living in her car, she had been lucky enough to avoid some of the more horrible things that happened to homeless people. She never had to sell her dignity. The closest she had come was donating blood and that damn DNA test.

She had been lucky, finding menial jobs that didn't

require a permanent address. She knew how to stretch a dollar. And if she had starved to death or frozen in the middle of the night, she hadn't cared all that much.

Until Levi.

Skyla walked around the back of the house to look at the Christmas tree one more time. How foolish to believe that Christmas miracles came true. She had never received a miracle in her pathetic life. Except Emory and then Levi.

How was she ever going to get him out of her head when he was in her soul? She unplugged the lights on the tree. Darkness snapped it up. Fat snowflakes fell from the sky and landed on the branches.

She needed to leave before she threw herself in the river, so she quickly ran back to her car. The river would have the power to call her just like it had when she first found this house. For once, she wanted to win.

Shoving the key in the ignition, she kicked over the engine, then backed out of the driveway. She would be in another state by the time Levi returned and found her gone. She hadn't bothered with a note. He was a smart man. He would figure out she wasn't coming back.

The headlights swooped across Melvin's yard. He came charging out his front door, waving his arms. She slammed on the brakes.

Melvin hurried around to the driver's side and mimed for her to roll down the window.

"Melvin, what are you doing in that house? You could get hurt."

"Never mind that. I just got a call." He held up his cell

phone. "Kassidy and Grant's house is on fire. Levi is over there."

"Oh no. Is anyone hurt?"

"I think they got everyone out, but I'm not sure. Will you give me a ride? I'm too worked up to drive myself, but I can help at the scene. I used to be on the fire department. At a time like this, all hands are needed."

"Jump in. We'll go over."

Two fire trucks were parked right in front of the house. Several police cars with their flashing red and blue lights cut off access to the yard and the side street. Skyla parked by a row of large wooden sheds in a rainbow of colors. This must be the Topside Community where people stayed for the summer and then packed up the tent portion of their homes into those permanent shed structures.

"Is this the Topside?" she said.

"One and the same. It loses some of its charm in the winter." Melvin struggled out of the car.

She met him on the sidewalk. "What can we do?"

"I'm going to see if the firefighters need any extra hands. You should find Levi." Melvin hurried off, not waiting for her response.

She was the last person Levi wanted to see. She doubted her sisters wanted to see her either, but it was Kassidy's house. No matter how Kassidy or Maren or Bailey felt about her, Skyla didn't want anything to happen to her sister.

Levi stood paralyzed as the firefighters sprayed water on the house. Grant's house. He could have lost his other brother tonight. Rage burned as hot as the fire shooting out the window.

An older woman in a long wool coat pushed through the crowd, yelling.

"Kassidy, where are you? Bailey? Maren?"

The three women broke free from their spots on the sidewalk and ran into the woman's arms. He was pretty sure that wasn't a mother. Must be an aunt or friend.

He walked up to Grant who held Emma against his chest. Emma had her fist in her mouth and put her head on her daddy's shoulder.

"Are you okay?" That was a dumb question.

"Not a chance. That's my home, man." Grant's jaw clenched.

Emma started to cry.

"Do you want me to hold her a second?"

Grant arched a brow. "We're fine."

The firefighters shut off their water. Puddles formed around the house as if the ocean had leaped over the dunes and drenched the road. The captain walked over.

"Grant, I can't be sure just yet, but my guess is the fire started at the Christmas tree. We put out the fire quickly. The damage seems contained to the front left corner. We'll know more in the morning. I'm sorry."

"Do you have any idea who's doing this, Kevin?" A vein pulsed in Grant's neck.

"Serenity's arson investigator is working with local law

enforcement to find out just that. Do you have any security cameras on the property?"

"No. It's Serenity. Everyone knows everyone else here."

"The arsonist is counting on that," Captain Wright said. "I will be honest with you. Man to man. Arson is a tough one to investigate. Evidence is often destroyed, and in this case every scene looks like the guy is just using paper as kindling. Real trees go up in seconds. That's why at the Christmas tree lot we give out a list of ways to prevent fire."

"If you had a witness, that would help," Levi said.

"It would be a place to start. We've got no motive except this person hates Christmas. I wish I had better news. I really do. I'll be in touch." Captain Wright nodded, then walked away.

"How am I supposed to tell Kassidy they may never catch who destroyed the home we built? I was supposed to keep my family safe, and I wasn't even home."

"Hey, you had no idea a fire had started. Everyone is safe. You're lucky."

Grant's face crumpled, and Levi's knees buckled. He had never seen Grant cry. Not even when Emmett died. He took Emma from Grant, then pulled him into a one-armed hug. Grant resisted at first, but he sank against him and sobbed. Emma squirmed in his arms, then began to cry again too.

"It's going to be okay," he said for the benefit of all three of them. Everything had to be okay. They had been through worse. "What can I do to help?"

"I don't know." Grant pushed away and swatted at his

face. "Don't tell Kassidy about this. But thanks. I'm glad you're here. I need my brother."

"I need mine too." Tears burned his eyes, but he held them back. Instead, he planted a soft kiss on Emma's head. She returned the favor but kissed his eye.

"Grant." Maren hurried over. "I just spoke with Shane. You three will stay with us. We have more than enough room in that big house. I'm going to take Kassidy to get some essentials for you all, then head over. It's late. Everyone needs some rest."

"Thanks." Grant kept his gaze on the house.

"Hello, Levi. Why are you holding my niece?" Maren glanced at him from the corner of her eye.

"Maren. I see I'm still at the top of your favorite person list. And by the way, she's my niece too."

"Did you put Skyla up to lying?" Maren's words snapped at him with sharp teeth.

"I—"

"He didn't put me up to anything, Maren. He was as blindsided as you." Skyla walked up to them. "Grant, I'm so sorry."

"Thanks."

"I want to know why you lied to us?" Maren fisted her hand on her hip. "What is it you're after? Because we don't have anything. We're not rich. Our father had nothing at the end of his life."

"I'll be happy to talk to you about my paternity at another time. Right now, let's focus on Grant, Kassidy, and Emma."

"Like we would accept help from you. Did you start this fire, Skyla?"

"Me? Why would I start a fire in my sister's house?"

"You didn't tell anyone you were our sister and those fires started after you showed up. Maybe it's you."

"That's enough, Maren." He stepped in front of Skyla to keep Maren at a distance. "Skyla is not the arsonist."

"How do you know? You claim not to know she was another one of our father's bastard children."

"Wow." Grant took Emma from him.

"Maren, take a deep breath. Skyla isn't the enemy." He may be hurt by what Skyla had done, but he would not allow Maren or anyone to accuse her of something she didn't do. She had been in his bed when Melvin's tree caught.

"Says you. Let me have Emma." Maren put her hands out to Grant, but he didn't give up his child. "The crib at my house is ready. This way you can take your time here and come back whenever. We'll keep the door unlocked for you." Maren turned to him. "I don't care what you say about Skyla. Even if she isn't the arsonist, she lied to everyone."

Grant hugged Emma. "I need to talk to Kassidy."

Levi gripped Grant's arm. "The money from the songs. I have it all. I saved it."

"I don't want that money."

"Take it for Emma, you stubborn pain in the ass." But he said it with a smile because things with Grant had taken the turn he had hoped for.

They didn't need any big conversation. They dealt with

their problem the way they knew how. Things would be better between them from now on. He was just sorry it took a fire in Grant's house to mend their fences.

"I need to talk to my wife." Grant and Maren slipped into the dwindling crowd, leaving him alone with Skyla.

"I'm glad everyone is okay," Skyla said.

"Me too. Look, you don't have to hang around here. I'll wait to see if Grant needs anything. You should go back to the cottage."

"I'm not staying. I was getting ready to leave when Melvin came running out of his house and yelling about the fire. He wanted to come over and help." Skyla pointed to Melvin having words with Captain Wright.

"That's it then." He wanted to pull her close because his feelings hadn't changed, but he didn't know if he could trust what she said any longer. She had left out an important part of who she was, and he couldn't figure out why.

"I guess so. Thank you again for everything. It was nice to feel like a normal person even if it was just a short time. Take care of yourself." She turned to leave.

He grabbed her hand and pulled her back. "Wait. Can we talk for a minute?"

Before Skyla could answer him, that older woman who was hugging the Russo sisters earlier ran over to them.

"I'm sorry to interrupt. My name is Joanna Russo. You must be Skyla."

Skyla's eyes narrowed. She crossed her arms over her chest. "Yes."

"And you're Levi Hawkins," Joanna said.

"That's right. I'm sorry. Have we met?" He had never seen this woman before tonight. He was certain of it.

"Not officially. Maren, Kassidy, and Bailey are my nieces. My brother Joe's girls. Kassidy has told me you're Grant's brother." Joanna touched the ends of Skyla's hair and smiled. "You look so much like Joe."

Skyla moved closer to him. He linked his fingers through hers, hoping she would understand he was there for her even if he couldn't say it.

"I know the timing is bad, but I didn't know you were here until just now. Could we talk?" Joanne held Skyla's gaze as if he weren't standing there at all.

Skyla glanced up at him.

"I think you should," he said. "I'll stay nearby, if you want." He would protect her, if she wanted it, even if they couldn't be together.

"Okay. We can talk. Back at Levi's cottage on River Road. It's the last one near the trees."

"I know the street well. I'll meet you there. Thank you, Skyla." Joanna glided back to her nieces.

"You're going to learn about your dad."

"I'm not sure I want to any longer. What difference will it make? I can't have the family I dreamed about. Having more information might just hurt worse."

"Why didn't you tell me? Please make me understand."

"I should have. I know that, but I wanted Bailey to like me first before I told anyone. And then I had decided not to tell at all. I thought being friends with her would be enough because who would want a homeless person as a sister?"

"You didn't give her a chance. She would have proved your worries wrong. But me, Skyla? After all we've shared, you still couldn't tell me that those women were your sisters?"

She stepped away from him and stared at the house with its burnt side. Broken and whole, like all of them.

"Have you ever been so afraid you make all the wrong choices?" She glanced at him, then away.

"We're all afraid." He hadn't known he had been afraid in his life until his diagnosis. Once that reality had set in, he could pick out all the other times fear had snuck up on him and how he had reacted.

"No. Not regular fear. Like the warnings in your head not to go into a wooded area at night. The kind of fear that stops your brain from working. The kind of fear that tears at your insides until there's nothing left. Did you feel that way when you found out you had cancer?"

"I did. But I used that fear to move me forward."

"Well, you're lucky because that kind of fear has derailed me over and over. And that was the fear that stopped me from telling Bailey the truth. And you."

"But I don't understand. You told me about Emory. Why not this?"

"Because Emory was the before in my life. She was the part of my life when things were good and sweet and whole. Learning I had a sister through a DNA test when I only took the test to make a few bucks so I wouldn't starve to death, is a part of the after. And the after has frightened me every single day."

"I would never have guessed you were that terrified since I met you."

She offered a lift of her shoulder.

"What happened that changed you since you've been in town?"

"You, dummy. You."

Chapter Twenty-Five

"I'll be at Melvin's. We're going to sit in the backyard. Take your time. Call when you're done, but please don't leave until we have a chance to talk." Levi stood on the front porch with her. Joanna waited inside. His lids were heavy and his face sallow. He looked as tired as the aching fatigue in her bones.

Fat snowflakes drifted down and disappeared as they hit the ground. If it wasn't for the glow of the porch lights capturing their descent, she would not have noticed them at all. She never liked winter until she came here.

They had returned to the cottage after Levi had one more chance to speak with Grant. Skyla had kept her distance. Maren had shot her enough looks to set her on fire too. Maren believed Skyla capable of arson. Others in town felt the same way. That fear she had told Levi about slithered up her throat. Any kind of safety seemed out of reach.

"I won't leave until we talk," she said.

"Go learn about your dad. Maybe finding out some stuff will help you heal." He kissed the top of her head.

She watched, holding off the inevitable, until he was in front of Melvin's before going inside. The cottage was warm. Joanna moved around in the kitchen as if she'd been there a hundred times. She hummed a Christmas tune as she poured water into mugs.

"I hope you like tea. I needed something to do with my hands." Joanna glided into the living room with two steaming mugs. "Shall we sit?"

They each took an end of the sofa and faced each other. Skyla was grateful for the furniture that made the house more of a home. They still had a long way to go... Levi had a long way to go, but the place was livable for now.

"I don't know what to say." She had no idea where to begin or what questions to ask. After all this time, she never believed she would understand her father.

"I knew about you." Joanna sipped her tea.

"You did?"

"Joe came to me after your mother told him she was pregnant."

"She said she never told the man who fathered me." She had asked a hundred times in a hundred different ways, hoping her mother would remember something or slip on a secret she held, setting it free. But her mother had always told the same story.

"You'll have to ask her about her choice not to reveal him, but she did find Joe. It wasn't too hard. He never left that tavern."

"I can't ask her. She passed away more than a decade ago."

Leaving Skyla alone in the world. If her mother had told the truth, she might have found her sisters sooner. She could've had a family all along, someone to hold her hand after Emory.

"I'm so sorry, dear. That must've been hard." Joanna leaned over and patted her knee. Joanna's hand was cold through the cotton of Skyla's pants.

"Losing her was hard. I had no one else for a long time until I met my husband."

"So, you're married?"

She told Joanna the whole story of her time with Will, losing Emory, and the divorce because everything should be left on the table now. Joanna put down her mug, then folded Skyla into a warm embrace.

"You poor thing. You have suffered far too much. How have you done it?"

"I don't know." And she didn't know. Every day was a new challenge and some harder than others. But since arriving in Serenity by the Sea, some of the grief muted. She had believed she deserved a chance at happiness, but maybe she didn't because she hadn't been honest.

"Did my father want me?"

Joanna smoothed her hands over her thighs. "Joe was a complicated man who enjoyed the company of women. While he was married to Maren and Kassidy's mother, he had an affair with Bailey's mother."

"I didn't know that."

"That's because you're new here. But anyone who has spent decades in Serenity knows the story. Joe divorced his first wife and married Bailey's mother. They split up too.

My brother liked women but didn't always choose the best mates for himself. Sorry to say. Both of those women weren't winning any awards for mother of the year. The girls all ended up living with Joe eventually."

Her mother had issues as well. Beverly had tried to be a good mother to Skyla, but her luck always seemed to be on the opposite end of good.

"Your mother showed up right before Thanksgiving that year and told Joe the news. I remember her. Young with the same red hair as you. I don't know what she was hoping for, but Joe was in the middle of divorce number two with three small girls and a mountain of bills. He wasn't in a position to be a father again and told her so. He told her to find someone better than him."

"So, it wasn't just a one-night thing."

"It was a summer love. Plenty of people come to town, hoping the ocean, salt air, and sun-kissed skin will deliver them a summer romance. I think your mother was hoping for that. Joe wanted companionship during a difficult time. They were careless about protecting themselves. He never planned on building a relationship with Beverly. I am sorry to have to tell you that, but at the time, I would have said Beverly felt the same way. She had plans. At least she had said she did. But with your arrival, everything changed I suppose."

"He didn't want me."

"I believe he did. He confided in me right before he passed that he regretted sending your mother away. That he had tried to find her but never could. He had hoped she'd

261

come back, but she never did. He wished he had known your name."

"Why didn't he try harder to find me?"

"My dear, Joe fought his own set of demons. We weren't raised in these modern times of talking about feelings. We were abandoned by our mother. Joe was just an infant. We never saw her again and he never recovered from that. Our father did his best to love us, but he was a cold man with an iron fist. Joe struggled right until the end. When life made something difficult for him, he avoided it."

"I wasn't worth trying for. I would have moved heaven and earth for my daughter. Nothing would have stopped me. I can't believe he wouldn't do the same."

"You're a stronger person than he was. He wouldn't have survived if one of the girls had died before him. He could barely handle everyday life, never mind a tragedy. He had mental health problems. Some day we can talk more about that if you want."

She wanted to close her eyes and sleep for a week. This conversation was too much. Her father hadn't wanted her. He hadn't thought he was good enough or worth enough to father another child. He had never considered for once what that child might need from him.

"Was he a good father to the others?"

"He did his best. He loved his children, and he would've loved you too if he hadn't been so frightened it paralyzed him."

She sucked in a breath. That fear she had told Levi about. Fear like a predator, lurking in the shadows, waiting to attack and take life blood. She shouldn't judge Joe so harshly, and yet she did. He was her father. She had deserved a man who would have fought for her, given her a chance to have a life with him. He had loved and supported his other three children. Why not her? Because his relationship with her mother had meant nothing to him?

"I don't think I can talk about this anymore tonight. I appreciate you coming here and sharing what had happened between my mother and Joe, but honestly, I almost wish I didn't know. I wish I had never taken that test."

"Well, I'm glad you did. And I'm glad you had the courage to come to town and find your sisters. They'll come around. Even Maren. You'll see. She's got a tougher shell because she's the oldest and found herself in the mother role more times than she should have been. But she's soft under there." Joanna pointed to her heart.

"Maren will never like me." And she wasn't so sure she would ever like her.

Joanna stood. "Give it time. Give yourself time. And if you can find it in your heart, give your father the grace he might not deserve."

"I don't know what to do."

"Build your life back up. Do it right here in Serenity. There are plenty of wonderful people in this town. Your sisters are here. In case you haven't noticed, Levi is in love with you."

"I doubt that." But he had said it before he found out she withheld a truth from him.

"Trust an old woman. Find yourself again, Skyla, my dear. You've earned it." Joanna shrugged into her coat.

"I'm staying with Bailey and Jack. Help me." Joanna tilted her head toward the ceiling and rolled her eyes. "It's going to be a houseful for the time being. But honestly, I love the noise, and I miss my family. You're my family now too. Don't you stay away from me."

"Where do you live? I haven't even asked you one question about you."

"We can talk about me another time. I'm moving back to Serenity. I haven't told anyone yet. I miss it here. I miss my ties to the beach. I haven't figured out where yet. Maybe I'll buy that empty house next door."

"You would make a great neighbor. I could use someone in my corner. I have to find a job and a place to live. I'm still in the exact spot I was when I got here."

"Not true. You have Levi. You're staying here. At least for now. A job will show up." Joanna wrapped her arms around her and gave a squeeze.

"You're going to be just fine. Everything will work out.

"How can you be so sure?"

"Because it always does."

Chapter Twenty-Six

Skyla plugged in the Christmas tree by the river. The lights snapped on, casting a white glow in that little corner. The small snowflakes continued to fall in lazy drifts. The brine of the river assaulted her nose. She didn't care. The ocean was magnificent, but River Road was her favorite place in Serenity. The river was a calmer companion and had provided her a place for renewal.

"She's pretty when she's lit up, but not as pretty as you." Levi's voice interrupted her thoughts. He walked toward her from the front yard. "I looked for you in the house."

"Yeah... I came outside."

She had sent a text after Joanna left to tell him he could have his house back. Then Skyla came out here to enjoy the view and process the things she had learned about her father. She had spent her life without knowing a single thing about the man who fathered her, and yet knowing he had turned her mother away when he found out his child was on the way cut deep into the armor she tried to keep around her heart. She wanted to understand his point of view, how worried he might have been about providing for a future for another child, or how his own doubts about himself led him to believe he wasn't a good father. But she didn't understand completely. She had once been a child who needed her father to protect her. And then she had become a woman who needed her father to continue to protect her from the bad things in the world.

Levi stopped a few feet short of her. She wanted to slip into his arms, tell him everything Joanna had said, but she remained planted in her spot. Relying on Levi could not continue.

"I shouldn't give the arsonist a reason to return, but I wanted to see the tree lit one more time. You were right not to put the tree inside." She would never have forgiven herself if Levi's house had caught fire.

"I wish I wasn't." He pushed his hat further onto his head. "I never realized how warm my hair kept my head. I think I might grow it back."

She laughed in spite of the recent events. She wasn't sure she would ever laugh again, but Levi did have a way about him. "I'm sure you have very nice hair."

"We'll see."

"You'll see." She wouldn't be around to see what he looked like with hair. She had no doubt it would only look great.

"Are you really leaving? Where will you go?"

"I don't know. I need to find a job. A job I can keep and grow with. I don't want day work or cleaning toilets.

a blessing."

"You could continue to fix up my house."

"I don't think so. I can't use you any longer."

"I shouldn't have said that. I'm sorry. I was hurt."

"You might have been right. You were the first person in a long time to offer me any kind of help. Of course, I would take it and then some. I don't get many opportunities. If you hadn't helped me, would I have stuck around?"

"I'd like to think you would have fallen for me anyway." He gave her a lopsided smile.

"I'll admit, you're charming." If he hadn't offered her a place to stay, she might not have continued her quest to meet Bailey. "Thank you. I'm not sure if I said that at all. Even though things didn't work out, I still got to meet my sisters."

"I don't want you to go."

"I can't stay. Everything is ruined."

"What if I buy another house and you fix that one up? Then I won't live there, and you won't even have to see me."

"What house would you buy?"

"I could buy the one next door." He hooked a thumb over his shoulder.

"Joanna joked about buying it too."

"Well, she can't have it. I'll outbid her. If I buy it, will you fix it up? You can live in it while you do."

"I don't know, Levi. I've made too many things complicated now."

He closed the distance between them. "How I feel about you is not complicated. I don't like that you hid your

267

Though, a job in housecleaning or office cleaning would be

identity from me. But I understand now why you did it. I didn't tell Grant about my cancer. I have no place to judge. Melvin helped me realize tonight that I was keeping score. You had a right to your secret. I don't want to lose you now that I found you."

"Melvin is a smart man."

"He is. He also thinks he knows who's setting the fires, which I'll tell you about, but let me say one thing first. Skyla, from the moment I saw you, I knew you had to be in my life. I couldn't explain it. Didn't even want to. I just wanted to be near you. And when I was, I wanted more. When you and I made love, I knew in that moment I could never let you go."

"Levi—"

"Please hear me out. I'm a risk-taker. At least I was before the cancer. I don't live by a lot of rules. They don't suit me. Falling for you was a risk I hadn't planned on during a time I thought I was done with risk."

"I'm not a risk-taker."

"Let me be for both of us. We have a good thing as long as we stay honest with each other. I have the ability to help you out until you're on your feet. If after the ground under you is solid and you don't want a relationship with me, walk. I'll understand. But don't leave now. Not before we've had a chance together."

"You're being more than generous. I don't have anything to offer you in return except maybe the promise to always tell the truth."

"Being with you reminded me of who I was and showed me who I want to be. I don't need anything except you."

"Can I think about it? I might still want to take a room at the boarding house." She wanted to be careful about how much she allowed Levi to take care of her. But she still needed money and a job. Without those, her car was her only place to live.

"Think about this. I love you, Skyla. I don't care how crazy that sounds. I didn't get to where I am in this life because I played it safe. I love you. You don't have to love me back, but I hope you will." He kissed her, slow and tender at first, then with an impatience and heat that made her tremble.

He rubbed his thumb over her lip. "Stay the night."

She held his intense gaze. If she spent the night in his arms, she would never want to leave. And if she didn't leave now, she might always wonder if her feelings for him were real or fed into by desperation.

"Levi, I'm afraid."

"Would you believe me if I said I am too?"

"If you say you are, you are."

"Then take a chance on me. You've got nothing to lose."

A month ago, that was true. But now... now she had plenty to lose all over again.

"Just stay the night. Worry about tomorrow in the morning." He twirled the ends of her hair between his fingers.

She took his hand in hers.

Then led him inside.

Chapter Twenty-Seven

Levi knocked on Maren's front door. The sun reflected off the ocean and blinded him when he looked east. Maren lived in an impressive home with an ocean view. She must be doing all right.

The heavy wooden door opened. Levi expected to see Maren glare at him. Instead...

"Holy cow, Shane Sutherland." Only the most infamous baseball manager in history.

"One and the same. You are?"

"Levi Hawkins. Grant's brother. He said I could stop by. I wanted to see how everyone's doing, and I was hoping to speak with Maren." Levi shook Shane's hand.

Shane stepped back to let him in. "They're all in the kitchen. So, you're a baseball fan."

"I am. It's great to meet you. Do you live here?" He had read online that Shane had left the team he managed in New York and had moved south, but Levi hadn't realized that meant Serenity by the Sea.

"You are new in town. I'll let Grant catch you up, but Maren and I are engaged."

That explained the house. "Good for you."

Grant stepped into the foyer. His hair was a mess and dark half circles hung under his eyes. He was in the clothes he had on last night. "Thought I heard you."

"Just wanted to check on you. I should've brought coffee."

"Coffee's in the kitchen. I'll leave you two brothers. I've got a few calls to make. Nice to meet you, Levi." Shane went through a doorway on the left.

"I've got some good news," Grant said.

"That's great to hear. You could use some."

"Our neighbor, Josephine—"

"The nosey one that watches out the window?"

"Yes, her. I never thought her being a busybody would come in handy, but she might have seen someone going into the front of the house while Kassidy and her sisters were in the back. She's going to talk with the arson investigator today."

"Well, look at that. I can't believe someone just walked in off the street, knowing the women were right outside. That's some balls. And what about Emma? Was she asleep in her room?"

Grant ran his hand through his hair. "I don't like to think about that. We got lucky there. We have a video monitor for her. Kassidy had it with her outside. No one went in that room."

"Something to be thankful for."

"Yeah, because if this guy had and I find out who is he, I'll kill him."

"I know that's anger talking." But if he were Grant, he'd feel the same way.

"You know what I mean." Grant dropped down on the bottom step of the wooden staircase.

"So, now what?"

"We wait to see if Josephine knows anything that can help, I guess."

"Can I do anything for you?" He leaned on the railing.

"I'm good. My family is safe. Would you want to catch a beer tonight, though?"

"I'd like that. A lot."

"I can't get used to you with a bald head." Grant stood.

Maren hurried into the foyer still wearing her pajamas. "Your voices carry. Did you know that?"

"Hello, Maren," Levi said. "I was hoping to talk to you for a minute."

Grant arched his brow. "Do you need backup?"

"Hey." Maren shoved Grant.

"We'll be okay." He wasn't here to fight with Maren or anyone. And Shane seemed like a pretty cool guy. Maren couldn't be all bad.

Grant gave him a hug. "I'll text you later."

Levi could not believe how his life had turned around. And all it took was getting cancer.

"What's up, Levi? Did you come here to plead Skyla's case? I know she's living with you."

"I did, in fact. She's great. She's had a tough life and made mistakes, but you should give her a chance."

"Why? Because you said so? We know your track record for the truth."

"If Grant can forgive me, and he's the only one who had a right to be mad at me, then you can give me a break too. Talk to her, Maren. She's a lot like you. Tough."

Maren crossed her arms and looked at the ground before looking at him. "I don't trust her."

"She's staying in town with me."

"Then I guess Shane and I will not be at Kassidy's for Christmas."

"Have it your way. But you're making a mistake. I'll show myself out."

He stepped onto the porch defeated. But at least he tried.

Chapter Twenty-Eight

Skyla poured grinds into the coffee maker. An early morning sun glistened against the river and shot prisms through the kitchen window. The outside of the window needed to be cleaned, but that would wait until spring. No point in her starting that project now when so many others needed her attention.

Levi was still asleep. He had come home late last night after meeting Grant for a beer but would be up soon and heading over to Melvin's. Melvin had narrowed down his suspicions on who the arsonist was to three people. Not as helpful as she and Levi had hoped, but there was still a chance with Josephine's testimony.

She had decided in the midst of their lovemaking two nights ago that she would take a risk with her heart and stay. Being with Levi wouldn't be hard. But seeing Bailey, Kassidy, and Maren around town would be difficult. She wasn't sure she could pull that off.

Working around the house with Levi would keep her

mind and her hands busy, but she needed to find a job that earned her money from someone other than the man in her bed. She couldn't find herself in a situation where she had no way to make a living. If things didn't work out with her and Levi, then she'd be in trouble again.

She opened the back door and let the cold fresh air wash over her and blow her hair away from her face. The smell of woodsmoke drifted by. Hopefully, the arsonist had not set another fire. She closed the door in haste, then returned to her brewing coffee.

Levi had contacts in New York City that was only an hour away by train ride. She wouldn't have to use her car to get back and forth and that was a blessing. He might be able to get her job as an assistant of some kind. He also left open the offer to work for him. She would only use that option as a last resort. An assistant in New York had a nice ring to it. She'd like to try that hat on for a little while.

The rich coffee aroma filled the kitchen. Christmas was only a few days away. For the first time in a long time, she had something to celebrate—her change in fortune. She touched her necklace. "We're going to be okay," she whispered into the room.

A knock came at the front door, startling her. She debated on waking Levi but decided he could use the rest and went to the front door. Her front door.

The frosted glass showed the silhouette of a woman. Of the four most likely options, she crossed her fingers it wasn't Maren.

With a glance over her shoulder and hope that Levi would appear on his own, Skyla opened the door to Bailey.

Bailey stood on the porch in her white cropped puffer jacket and matching knit cap with pom-pom. She held a cardboard tray with three to-go cups. Her eyes were red as if she were recently crying.

"Hi," Bailey said. "I hope you don't mind my barging in unannounced. I came to apologize."

"You have nothing to apologize for."

"I kind of do. Can I come in? It's freezing out here."

Skyla moved aside to allow Bailey to pass. "Let's go in the kitchen."

"This place is cute." Bailey put the tray on the table.

"It's got good bones. Still needs a lot of work."

"Does Levi know that living room furniture is too big for that room?" Bailey leaned in like a conspirator and nodded her head toward the front of the house.

"I believe he does." The furniture was growing on her. She would find a way to make it work.

"I brought coffee from the bookstore. Jack is trying out this new brand to see if he wants to sell it. You guys can let me know what you think." Bailey removed the cups from the tray.

She nodded because words stuck in her throat. Bailey stood in her kitchen. Progress.

"Look, I'm sorry, Skyla. I overreacted. I shouldn't have. I don't know what's gotten into me lately. It's the store expansion and Jack and... well, whatever. I've behaved badly. I hope you can forgive me." Bailey dragged her hat off her head.

"I should've told you right away that we were sisters. I was afraid you'd reject me if you knew I was homeless."

"I'm not like that. If you had shown up on day one and said we were sisters and you needed a place to live, I would have been the most likely of the three of us to give you a bed."

"I have no doubt that is true. But I wasn't looking for a handout."

"I would have helped you."

"I didn't want your help. I wanted a sister." And a place to belong.

"Can we start over?"

"Why do you want to do that?"

"I spoke with Aunt Joanna after she left here. I'm so sorry, Skyla. You have been through hell and back. You need someone in your corner. Let me be that person." Tears sprung to Bailey's eyes.

"I don't know, Bailey. I appreciate what you're saying, but Kassidy and most definitely Maren don't want me around."

"Kassidy wanted to come with me this morning and bring you a bucket of sea glass, but I asked her to let me come alone to apologize."

"You can stop apologizing. Tell her thank you. I'd like to see the sea glass. But what about Maren?"

"Maren is a lot of bark. Don't listen to what she said to Levi. I'll talk with her and Aunt Joanna plans on speaking with her too."

"Levi? When did he speak with her?" Levi hadn't mentioned seeing Maren over the last day or when he went to visit Grant. But Skyla should've known Maren would be there.

"I saw her when I stopped by the house yesterday." Levi stood in the entryway in a flannel shirt and jeans. His stubble had thickened during the night, giving him a grizzly look she liked. "I'm sorry I didn't mention it."

"Why didn't you?"

"Because I couldn't convince her to give you a chance and I didn't want you to feel badly about that."

"Wow. You are a different person." Bailey handed him a to-go cup. "I like the bald head. Are you losing your hair and decided to end the relationship first?"

"Had cancer."

Bailey gave a nod as if Levi had spoken of the weather. "Good enough reason. Drink the coffee. Tell me what you think."

He took a sip. "Pretty good."

"I'll tell Jack."

"I'll let you two ladies finish up here. I'm headed to Melvin's. Thanks for the coffee."

Skyla gripped his arm. "Thank you for having my back."

He placed a kiss on her lips, then went out the front door.

"Yowza. Jack doesn't even look at me like he wants to devour me." Bailey giggled.

Skyla's laugh relieved her dry throat like water poured on the cracked earth. She wanted to laugh like this with her sister forever.

"I'd like to give you your job back. The grand opening for the new edition is right after Christmas. I could really use the help."

"I don't know." She was afraid to take another chance.

"Please, Skyla."

She had wanted to be brave for a long time now. And being brave meant being scared and doing that scary thing anyway. Bailey waited for her answer. Her hands pressed together as if in prayer.

"Well? Will you?"

"Yes."

Chapter Twenty-Nine

Christmas morning brought more gray skies, but Skyla didn't care if it rained all day. She wished she and Levi could be snowed in, but no snow was in the forecast.

She had been up for hours making French toast for breakfast. It used to be Emory's favorite meal and now Skyla wanted to share it with Levi.

She had a couple of presents for him too. Nothing fancy, but she wanted him to have something to open from her on their first Christmas together. This afternoon they were invited to Bailey and Jack's where everyone would gather, including Aunt Joanna. Kassidy and Grant usually hosted, but not this year. Maren and Shane were not coming.

Skyla tried not to focus on Maren's absence. She hoped some day they could be friends. That would be another Christmas miracle for another day.

"Good morning." Levi wrapped his arm around her waist from behind and pulled her to him.

She snuggled her back against his front. "Merry Christmas."

"Merry Christmas to you. I see you've been busy."

"I hope you like French toast."

"I'll like anything you make. Grant just texted me. They have news on the arsonist."

She whipped around to look at him. "Really? What is it?"

The new doorbell she installed by herself chimed. They looked at each other.

"Who could that be?" Levi went to the door. Skyla followed.

She held her breath as he opened the door. They weren't expecting anyone. Melvin stood on the porch in his blue coat with a scarf wrapped around his neck and up to his nose.

"Merry Christmas." He came inside. "Hope you don't mind me barging in, but I wanted you to know first. I'm moving in with my daughter. I've sold my house."

"You did?" she asked.

"Craziest thing. A buyer came out of nowhere. Offered me three times what it's worth. I hate to leave our street and you two, but I couldn't pass up the offer." Melvin handed them a gold gift bag. "Something to celebrate later. Put it on ice. I'll be back. I've got to run. Merry Christmas."

She closed the door. "That was weird."

"I'll say." Levi pulled out a bottle of champagne from the bag. "Go, Melvin."

"I'll put that in the fridge. So, what about the arsonist? Do they know who it is?" There hadn't been any more fires since Kassidy and Grant's house. The whole town waited, holding their breath for an answer. "Please tell me it isn't Todd from the hardware store."

"It's not Todd."

"That's good. I think he'd make a good friend for you."

"Are you picking my friends now?"

"Just the one."

Levi choked out a laugh. "The arsonist isn't Todd, but it is... Kevin Wright."

"The captain of the fire department? Talk about crazy."

"I know. Josephine identified him. He cracked under the questions. Says he hates Christmas and Christmas trees. He picked his victims from the people who purchased from his lot and those he knew wouldn't be home. When he hit Grant and Kassidy's, he thought they were all still at the Christmas Under the Stars event. He's always hated Grant's success and the fact they built a two-story house on that street."

She dropped down on the sofa. "What a morning."

Levi sat beside her. "At least we have answers."

"I really thought it was Colin from the bookstore."

"It's always those you least expect," he said.

"I'll say."

"Can I change the subject?"

"Sure."

"I have something for you." He pulled out a small box wrapped in red from her stocking hanging on the mantel.

They had left their tree outside, but it was too cold to open presents out there, so she had purchased two stockings with their names inscribed. She hadn't known Levi placed something in hers.

Her hands shook as she took the box from him.

"Open it," he said.

She tore off the paper then removed the box's lid and found three silver keys inside. "I don't understand."

He took her hands in his. "I'm the person who bought Melvin's house. He doesn't know it was me. I'd like to keep it that way. I also bought the house next door. If you say yes, then I'd like to give your aunt this house and level the other two."

"And do what with the land?"

"Build our forever home. As big or as small as you'd like. Any way you'd like. I would only have one request."

"What request would that be?"

"Allow me to put a big Christmas tree in our front window."

"Levi, this is a lot. Are you sure?"

"I'm a risk-taker, remember? Will you build a future with me?"

She glanced around the room of their little cottage still in need of repair. She had come to this town with nothing and now had a path before her worth walking and a man worth loving. Her fingers toyed with her necklace. Her heart still ached and always would. She would always fight the guilt of living when her daughter never had the chance. What kind of a mother would she be if she didn't at least try to live her life? What would Emory want her to do?

"Skyla, what do you say? If I hold your hand, will you jump with me?"

She placed a kiss on his soft lips. Lips she wanted to kiss this Christmas and every other for as long as the Universe allowed.

"Yes, Levi. Yes, to our forever home. Yes, to taking a risk. Yes, to you and me."

~

But wait, there's more!

This is usually the place where I give you a sneak peek into the next book. Though I don't have a first chapter ready, there will be a Sea Glass Five releasing in 2026.

Make sure to follow my newsletter (Click Here) to keep up to date on all the details!

Thanks, Stacey

Acknowledgments

~

Over a year ago, at a readers' conference, I met a fantastic woman with a bright smile. We chatted about books and when I asked her name, she said, "Skyla-Mae." I fell instantly in love with it. Her name is a beautiful as she is. So I asked if I could use it for a character and she willingly indulged me. Though my character Skyla and the real Skyla-Mae are very different, the book's Skyla carries Skyla-Mae's name with pride. Thank you, Skyla-Mae. I hope I did your name justice.

I need to give a shout out to my friend, Todd Scherr. He made a joke once about having a walk-on part in a book. I couldn't let that go. Todd from the hardware store, and Levi's new friend, is inspired by my Todd. The similarities end with the name. Oh, well, also where I mention his wife Ellen. Todd does have a wife Ellen, and I adore her.

I will forever be thanking the incomparable Robin Rottner, my Content Editor. She asks all the right questions so I can make this book and every book the best possible.

My Executive Administrator, Joanne Gelderblom, weaves her magic on a daily basis and finds ways to give me time to write. I don't know what I would do without her.

Last, but never least, I must thank all of you, reading this book. Those two words are never enough. You bring my characters to life by believing in my story. Thank you for allowing me to give you an escape you must certainly deserve.

Read On!

xo

Stacey

Also by Stacey Wilk

Serenity Series

Sea Glass Made with Second Chances

Sea Glass Hidden in Plain Sight

Sea Glass Out of Balance

Sea Glass Wrapped in Red

Heritage River Series

The Risk for House and Home

The Bridge Between Love and Lies

The Essence of Whiskey and Tea

Hometown Series

Taking Root

Raising Winter

Defining Chances

Beginning Over

Steeling Hearts

Whispering Christmas

Winter at the Shore Series

No More Darkness

Through the Darkness

Light Upon the Darkness

The Brotherhood Protectors World

Winter's Last Chance

The Last Betrayal

Her Last Word

The Last Days of Christmas

Seduced by Denial

Chill in the Air

Fighting for Tessa

Nash's Promise

Cruz's Watch

Harlan Unleashed

Big Sky Country Series

Time Won't Erase

Stay Awhile

Love Never Ends

Dare to Tell

About the Author

From an early age, best-selling and award-winning author, Stacey Wilk, told tales as a way to escape. At six she wrote short stories in composition notebooks, at twelve she wrote a novel on a typewriter, in high school biology she wrote rock star romances in her binder instead of paying attention.

But it wasn't until many years later, inspired by her children and a looming birthday, that she finally took her storytelling seriously. And published her first novel in 2013. Since then, she's gone on to publish thirty-three more so women everywhere can indulge in books that hook them heart and soul.

She isn't done telling stories. Not by a long shot. If you want to read her emotional and honest books about family, romance, and second chances, visit her at www.stacey-wilk.com

To see what she writes next, follow her Facebook group for her amazing readers – Stacey's Novel Family https://bit.ly/2FK8Lae

Or join her newsletter - https://bit.ly/2AojEFk